Best-seller

"Charles, relax," my father said. "You'll meet someone, maybe not now. Maybe in college. If not in college, in medical school. You'll slim down. Adolescence is a time of trial and torment. People forget that. They only remember the good parts."

A time of trial and torment. Boy, that really hits it on the head. I like that. *The Adolescence of Charles A. Goldberg, A Time of Trial and Torment.* That sounds gripping. It could be a best-seller, if only it could end happily.

**Other Point paperbacks
you will want to read:**

A Band of Angels
  by Julian F. Thompson

When the Phone Rang
  by Harry Mazer

Breaking Camp
  by Steven Kroll

The Golden Pasture
  by Joyce Carol Thomas

Don't Care High
  by Gordon Korman

Misjudged
  by Jeanette Mines

point

GOING BACKWARDS

Norma Klein

SCHOLASTIC INC.
New York Toronto London Auckland Sydney

ISBN 0-590-40329-X

12 11 10 9 8 7 6 5 4 3   8 9/8 0 1 2/9

Printed in the U.S.A.   01

For Elena Schiffrin

GOING BACKWARDS

CHAPTER ONE

As I put the tape in the tape deck, I heard my grandmother's footsteps. She was slowly circling down the hall through my parents' bedroom, into the library. We have a gigantic apartment, which is partly why my father thought my grandmother could come live with us. She's been what he calls "disoriented" since my grandfather died a year ago; I guess he was afraid she wouldn't be able to manage alone in their condominium in Florida. My grandmother had been living there for about twenty years, ever since they moved from Riverdale where my grandfather had a furniture business.

I tried to tune out my grandmother's footsteps and the vague mumbling noises she makes when she does this routine. My parents were out at a dinner party and I was baby-sitting for my ten-year-old brother, Kaylo. Since I'm sixteen and a guy, baby-sitting isn't my normal pastime, but they pay me what they call "going rates." Still, it's not like I have a choice. Luckily, he was asleep already.

My twelfth-grade French teacher, Mlle Grazier, says my accent isn't that good. She suggested playing these records. You're supposed to repeat each phrase and then play it back to compare your accent to Monsieur X on the record. *"Je m'apelle Charles,"*

I repeated, feeling like a jerk talking aloud in the empty room. My voice is lower than it used to be, but when I try and speak French, it still does strange things. *"Je suis un étudiant. . . ."* Then I stopped, catching sight of my grandmother in the doorway. I pushed the stop button. "What do you want, Granny?" I asked. Dad — my grandmother is his mother — says to always talk to her in a soothing, quiet voice.

My grandmother crept into the room. She's little and kind of fragile-looking with white hair that stands up on end sometimes. She was in her bathrobe and slippers. She looked at me with her pale, blinking eyes. "I just want to ask you something," she said haltingly. "What is your father's name?"

"You mean Dad?" I knew who she meant, but it was hard to believe we were having this conversation again since we just had it about twenty minutes earlier.

"Your father," she repeated, as though "Dad" might be someone completely different.

"His name is Samuel . . . Sam."

"Oh." She leaned forward, swaying slightly. She's a little hard of hearing. "Would you repeat it?"

"Samuel."

My grandmother looked cautiously around the room. She came closer to my desk, lowering her voice confidentially. "That's why I haven't spoken to him in all these years," she whispered. "That's why. . . . He must think it's funny. . . . But I never knew where he was — Brazil or anywhere!" She threw up her hands in bewilderment. "I had no idea where he was!"

What's really strange about this to me is that every winter we used to visit my grandparents in Daytona Beach, where they had their house. I remember everything about it — the walks on the beach with my grandfather, how he would poke at man of war jellyfish with a stick, the mango and papaya drinks from the stand on the boardwalk, the way my mother always got obsessed that Kaylo would get a sunburn because he liked to run wildly up and down the beach (she calls him the "perpetual motion machine"). We always went for ten days in January; it was a perfect vacation. I liked it a lot better than summer camp, where you have to keep going from one activity to another. In Daytona Beach you could lie on the sand all day, or swim, or go snorkeling. Since it was a "family vacation," we'd all go out to eat at night. Sometimes we even went to fancy places with dancing. My parents love to dance, though they're both a little plump, or fat — to be unkind. In fact, everyone in our family could stand to lose a couple of pounds — all except my grandmother who is only five feet tall, and weighs around ninety pounds. She seems to shrink every day.

"Remember how we used to visit you, Granny?" I asked. "How we used to collect seashells together?"

She smiled, embarrassed. "I'm not sure."

I went to the closet. I still keep the best of my shell collection in a box in my closet. Mom says that, when I go to college, I have to start weeding out some of my collections. I collect comics and old issues of *Rolling Stone*, too. I took out one of the most spectacular shells. I've taken good care of them and they're still in just about perfect condition. "Remember the day we found that one?" I said. "You couldn't believe how lucky we were." I can remember everything about that moment — how hot it was, the blue bathing suit my grandmother was wearing. She always had a deep tan and wore her hair in little white curls. She still played tennis then, even though she was in her seventies. Maybe she couldn't run too fast even then, but if you hit it to her, she really walloped the ball. My grandfather didn't play. He wasn't much for sports. He used to walk along the beach or read the stock market page in the local paper.

She touched the shell with one finger. "Pretty."

"*You* found it," I tried to remind her. "*I* didn't even see it."

I hate to say this, but sometimes I'm not positive my grandmother knows who I am. She looked at me with an intent expression, as though I was a fact she'd forgotten for an exam. "You're a beautiful boy!" she suddenly exclaimed.

The fact is, I'm not what anyone would call beautiful — I'm overweight, wear glasses, and don't have terrific skin. Still, maybe all she meant was I was young and she was old. Who knows? "Are you getting tired?" I suggested. "You could go to sleep now." Kim, my best friend, was due to come over pretty soon to do homework with me.

My grandmother looked over her shoulder. "I can't go in there. A man is in there — a doctor."

"Sure, that's Dad. That's your son, Sam, the one we were talking about before. He's a doctor."

4

At that my grandmother beamed. "My son is a doctor!" she said.

"Right, he's a pathologist." That was probably dumb. She can't even remember who he is half the time, so why mention what kind of doctor he is? I doubt very strongly I'll ever be a doctor, but the last kind in the world I'd think of being is a pathologist. Half the time my father's doing autopsies to determine what someone died of. He likes to joke about the fact that at least malpractice suits are fairly rare — if you make a wrong move while cutting up a cadaver, it's kind of late in the day for the patient to complain. My father has a pretty grim sense of humor. Mom's the one who has the kind of personality people associate with fat people — jolly and open with a big booming laugh.

"I can't go in there," my grandmother said. "He'll kill me if I go in."

I think she got that idea because my father sometimes has consultations in his office and a couple of times my grandmother wandered in and scared the hell out of whoever was there. She's gotten the general idea that during the day that part of the house is off limits.

My grandmother's attitude toward my father is strange. She really worships him. I don't mean just love or even adoration. I mean she thinks he's God. That's funny because she has another child, my Aunt Rachel, but she doesn't seem to matter to her. When my grandmother sits next to my father and he tries to explain something to her, someplace she's supposed to go or something she's supposed to do, she looks at him like he'd just emerged from the

5

heavens. A couple of times I've seen her reach out while he's talking and touch the tip of his tie or his coat, the way someone might with the Pope. What makes it all weird is she's not religious. It was my grandfather who did what Mom calls "the whole Jewish bit": going to synagogue, having a Seder. Whenever my grandfather started talking about religion, my father and grandmother would exchange glances like they thought he was an idiot. Since Mom was raised as an agnostic, it doesn't matter much to her one way or the other.

Frankly, I wonder if this whole thing is going to work, having my grandmother live with us. Kaylo is pretty young to understand what's going on, but even our housekeeper, Josie, finds my grandmother kind of hard to take. Granny keeps accusing Josie of stealing her clothes, which is supremely unlikely on a million grounds — first, Josie would never steal anything and second, she's about four sizes bigger than my grandmother. I didn't want to be rude to my grandmother, but I wanted to get the French out of the way before Kim arrived. "I've got to work," I said, pointing to the tape deck.

"Yes, my sweetheart." My grandmother bent down and hugged me. I'm about a foot taller than her, almost six feet. Mom says I've doubled in height and bulk in the last year. Once a couple of months ago she came into the bathroom by mistake while I was taking a bath. She let out a gasp. I thought it might be something to do with how I looked naked, but she just said, "You're bigger than the bathtub! You used to be able to fit all those rubber animals in with you." It's been quite a while since

I've taken a bath with rubber animals, but maybe to my mother it seems more recent.

"I love you so much," my grandmother said, backing out of the room. "You'll never know how — "

"*Mais d'accord,*" the tape said. "*Si on peut —* "

"*Mais d'accord,*" I repeated, relieved to see her disappear out the door. "*Si on peut. . . .*" I've taken French for four years now and I read fairly fluently. The reason I'd like to get good at speaking is I've thought sometimes about joining the foreign service, being some kind of diplomat. I haven't broken this news to my parents. They're ardent amateur musicians — my father plays in a chamber group every Tuesday and my mother takes recorder lessons twice a week. They have their heart set on me or Kaylo becoming a "real" musician. I've taken voice lessons since I was eight, but to tell the truth, my heart's not in it. Maybe Kaylo will fulfill their dreams. He takes violin and piano and he's just in fifth grade.

Just as I was getting into the tape, my grandmother peeked into the room again. I thought if I kept on working she might just go away, but it made me nervous the way she stood there, staring at me, so I pressed the stop button again.

"I'm not going to bother you," she said timidly. "I know you have to work. You work very hard. I just want to know one thing. Tell me, what is your father's name?"

I couldn't believe it! I looked at her in silence for a moment. "Samuel," I said finally. "His name is Samuel."

"Samuel!" Her face lit up the way it did when I'd told her before that Dad was a doctor. "Would you believe it? Why, it's a revelation to me! My darling! All these years I never knew, would you believe it?"

"Well, now you know," I said.

"Yes . . . Samuel." She opened the large purse she carries around with her. It's stuffed with old bottles of pills and slips of paper my father writes on to remind her to take her pills, keep doctor's appointments. "Here," she said, fumbling around in the purse. "I'll get a piece of paper and write it down."

"No, that's okay, Granny," I said, walking over and closing her purse. "Never mind."

"All right," she said. She put her thin, soft hand on my arm. "Tell me, my pupishka, whose child are you? Rachel's?"

"No," I said. "I'm Charles, Megan's son. Your daughter-in-law. Rachel is your daughter."

My grandmother nodded and smiled, shaking her disheveled white hair back and forth. "Darling," she said. "I'm so grateful to you. When we get to New York, you'll come see me and — " She stopped and looked around the room. "This isn't my house. I don't usually live here. I just — "

"Yes, I know," I said, "but. . . ." Then I remembered one of my father's expressions. "It's going to be okay, Granny. Don't worry about a thing."

CHAPTER TWO

At around nine, Kim came over. Boy, was I glad to see him! The same thing that made my father think it would work to have my grandmother living with us is what makes me not like being here by myself. I have to admit I even like having Kaylo in the apartment with me, even when he's asleep and I know that awake, in an emergency, he'd be no help at all, more the opposite. To be alone in a twelve-room apartment with all those halls can be really spooky. It's not like I'm literally afraid of the dark or believe in ghosts. I just don't like the feeling of being alone. Kim's family consists of his parents, his two sisters, and his grandfather all living in four rooms, so he's always glad to come over here where it's quiet.

"So, how's it going? Did you get the French done?"

Kim's Korean; he has a mind like a steel trap. He's the best in our class in math and pretty good at everything else, too. He got offers from all the colleges he applied to, but picked Harvard. What he wants to be is a violinist, but in his case I'd bet he might actually make it. He practices a minimum of four hours a day. Our school, Diamond, is supposed to be for kids who excel or are interested

9

either in music, art, or one of the performing arts like dance.

"Well, I've had quite a few interruptions," I said ironically. Kim knows all about my grandmother. In a sense he can understand, since they live with his grandfather who's almost ninety and almost totally blind. But his grandfather's mind is excellent. You can talk to him about anything.

"You want to go over the calc? You said you weren't sure of some of the answers."

I don't know why I'm even taking calculus. I think it's basically because my father thinks it's important. He's afraid all I'll learn is stuff connected with the arts, and that I'm not good enough at singing to make it professionally. But I'm not sure if I could make pre-med, either. I'm not a whiz at science. Despite that, I got into Cornell on early decision, but I think that's partly because Dad went there.

We stretched out on the floor and put our papers side by side. I began searching for the problems that had given me trouble. A minute later Granny walked into the room. "I've just been wandering around and around," she said to no one in particular. "Around and around." She walked out the other door.

I jumped up nervously. "God, I swear I'm going crazy!" I said, breathing too fast. "She keeps coming in here every other minute!"

"She does look pretty bad," Kim agreed. "Maybe it's from having nothing to do." His grandfather goes to the senior citizens center during the day and teaches little kids to play the violin.

"But what can she do?" My voice cracked and went up an octave. "You tell her something and one second later she forgets."

"How about something to read?" Kim suggested.

"Her eyes are no good. She can't."

"Maybe you could get her some beads to string," Kim said. "That's what they do at the center. They give them things to do that are mechanical, that don't take a lot of brain power."

I laughed grimly. "She'd probably just drop the beads all over the floor or cut her fingers or something."

"It's really that bad?" Kim asked.

I sat down again, trying to get a grip on myself. "It's so depressing to see her wandering around the way she does."

Kim looked down at the calc problems again. "Well, I guess there's no point in worrying if there's nothing you can do."

We got a little work done, but about fifteen minutes later I heard that familiar creaking down the hall. Kim looked at me with a slight smile. "I think she's coming back again."

"Shit." I started laughing involuntarily.

"I can see her," Kim whispered. He nudged me. "There she is."

My grandmother stood in the doorway, sighed, and said something incomprehensible. Then she walked around the room and out the door, as though we weren't there.

"See, that's what *always* happens! She starts muttering under her breath. I can't even understand what she's saying."

"I understood it," Kim said. One reason he's so good at music is he has perfect pitch and can hear anything.

"What'd she say?"

"She said, 'I'm so tired of going around, I'm ready to plotz.' Something like that, anyhow."

I sat up again. Even though having Kim there made a big difference, I still felt rattled. "What's weird is, she knows she's doing it and she doesn't stop. Why doesn't she sit down and be quiet?"

"What could she do?" Kim asked. "Stare at the wall?"

"I don't know. She could do something."

"She could go to sleep," Kim said. "Hey, how about that? Why not give her a sleeping pill?"

I laughed grimly. "She gets around five a night as it is. Plus about half a bottle of Valium."

We settled down to the work again. Then Kim got up to go to the bathroom. I noticed the shell I'd taken down earlier and stood up on the chair to put it back in its box. The closet was dark, quiet, and stuffy.

"Do you want anything, my darling?" I heard suddenly, right behind me. As I turned around with a start, the chair revolved under me, almost making me lose my balance. I grasped the edge of the shelf and looked down at my grandmother, who was standing there, holding a bowl of grapes. "You want some?" she asked, offering the dish to me.

"No," I said, my voice shaking. I climbed carefully down from the chair. "I don't want any!"

I walked quickly out of the room, through the hall, and into the study. I sat down in my father's big leather chair and dialed the number he'd left for me. Some man I didn't know answered. "Can I speak to Dr. Goldberg, please?" I said. "This is his son. It's an emergency."

A few minutes later my father's voice came on the phone. He has a very deep voice, which always sounds tired, like you'd just woken him up in the middle of a deep sleep. "What's up?"

"Dad, listen, it's Grandma. She's really just . . . she's driving me crazy. She keeps coming in here every second. I'm trying to study! I have an exam tomorrow."

"I put her to bed when I left," my father said wearily.

"Well, she got up again. She keeps asking who you are and where she is. I mean, look, if you want to pay me ten dollars an hour, it's one thing, but — "

"Did she wake Kaylo?"

"No." Sometimes I think that's all my parents care about. They've made a thousand jokes about raising the baby-sitter and then having the baby. Big joke.

"Charles, look, I know it's hard for you. It's hard for all of us. But we can't come home now. . . . Just give her two more Valiums and see how that works. They're in the bottle in our bedroom with the — "

"Yeah, I know." I was already feeling foolish for having panicked. "So, how's the party?"

"What?" My father sounded distracted.

"Are you having a good time at the party?"

"Counting the minutes." Mom says Dad's favorite evening is sitting by himself in his study, drinking red wine out of a water glass, and listening to Brahms.

I explained to Kim what Dad had suggested and went to get the pills. We found my grandmother sitting on her bed, staring out the window. "Granny," I said, "Dad said you should take these and go to bed."

She took the glass and obediently swallowed the pills. There was a pause. "Okay, you just go to sleep, Granny," I said, trying to imitate my father's bedside manner. "We'll be in there so don't worry."

We went into the kitchen to get a snack. I got out a salami and hacked off a few slices. "It's really terrible to get that old," Kim said, "if you don't have your mind intact."

"Yeah," I agreed. "It's funny. I used to worry about it a lot when I was a kid, but I don't so much anymore."

"My mother worries about it a lot," Kim said. "Not that she's *that* old."

"How old is she?"

"Forty."

"Mine's almost fifty. . . . They had us kind of late." I think one reason they were surprised to have Kaylo was my mother was thirty-nine at the time. I guess they figured their child-rearing years were over. A lot of times I wish they had been.

"Your mother doesn't look that old," Kim said.

It's true. Even though her hair is going gray,

Mom's kind of big and boisterous. When she laughs, you can hear it a block away. It used to bother me, but by now I'm used to it. She and her friend Portia run a catering service, which Dad thinks is a big mistake since all they do all the time is talk about or plan meals. She says *he* should talk. She thinks he's worse off because on top of being overweight, he's a chain smoker. Mom quit cold turkey eight years ago. "She's got a lot of energy," I said. "But I think this thing with my grandmother is getting on her nerves almost worse than on mine."

Kim looked puzzled. "Why?"

It's hard to explain things like this to Kim. In Asian families I guess it's so drummed into them to show respect for their elders, and for families to work together toward a common goal. He can't understand the average Jewish family where everyone is at each other's throats about the utmost trivia. "I guess she doesn't like the way Grandma worships my father. She thinks it's sick. She says doctors get enough adulation from their patients."

Kim listened patiently, but I knew he still didn't get it. "Have they ever thought of putting her in a home?"

"Maybe as a last resort. Dad is still hoping this will work."

Footsteps were coming down the kitchen hall. They made a different, softer sound on the linoleum than on the wood. A second later my grandmother was peering at us from the doorway. "Cookoo!" she said, smiling gleefully. She padded into the room, her pink nightgown hanging off her shoulders. She was holding the large glass filled with ice and grape juice that I'd given her to take her pills with. "Here," she said, thrusting the glass at me. "You drink that."

"No thanks, Granny," I said. "I'm not thirsty."

She glared at me. "Spoiled!"

"Oh, okay," I said. I took the glass from her and set it down in front of me. "I'll have some later."

"Drink it," she insisted. "It's good."

I took a sip. It was syrupy sweet. I set the glass down again. "Later," I said. "I'm not thirsty."

Seeming satisfied, she walked over to the sink.

"Want to go to sleep?" asked Kim.

"What?" My grandmother looked at him vaguely.

"Sleep?" he repeated, putting his head to one side.

"Oh yes, yes, in a minute," she said. She walked over and sat down in a chair next to us. "I'll just be a minute."

"That's okay, Granny," I said.

There was another pause. "You're still up," she said suddenly, frowning. "Why're you still up?"

I cleared my throat. "It's not late. It's only ten-thirty."

"No!" she protested. She looked at me slyly, like someone who knew when her leg was being pulled.

"Yes," said Kim. He reached over and put his finger on the clock. "That's the other hand, see?"

"Oh . . . yes." she nodded. "The people who live here know," she said in a slow, drifting voice. "A young doctor here . . . inside . . . his wife." Her voice trailed off.

"Yes, well, why don't you go to sleep now?" I suggested.

"Right," Kim repeated. "Sleep, okay?" He closed his eyes with a beatific expression.

"Yes," she said, getting up. "I'll go, I'll go."

When she had left, I began biting my thumbnail. When my mother quit smoking, I promised I'd stop biting my nails, but I didn't. She says it's just a matter of willpower, which is probably true. I just don't have any. "You're oral, like your father," she says. "Next it'll be smoking." Even Kaylo sucks his thumb. I guess it's a connecting family neurosis. "Sometimes I think she's going completely off her rocker," I said.

Kim nodded. "It is getting worse," he said. "You're right. How old is she, anyway?"

"Eighty-one. . . . But look at your grandfather. It's not just age."

"Something happens to the brain," Kim said, touching his head. "Cells disintegrate."

"Boy, I hope they find a cure before we're that age," I said. For some reason I can imagine me becoming like my grandmother more easily than I can imagine my parents being like that. I'm so disorganized already and I'm only sixteen!

Kim frowned. "Do you hear anything?"

We listened together. There was a sound, too faint to be distinguished, of a human voice rising abruptly, falling softer, rising again.

"She's talking to herself," I said.

"I wonder what she thinks about," Kim said. "Does she think she's alone?"

I shrugged. "Who knows?"

"It's a strange sound," Kim said.

17

"Yeah."

Then there was a dull thud and a moment of silence, followed by short cries. We ran in. My grandmother was sitting on the floor, her legs straight out like a child's. There were stains of purple on her nightgown and on her arms and legs. She kept rocking back and forth, making harsh guttural sounds that sounded like laughing. "Euh . . . euh gevalt," she said over and over.

"Granny!" I said, bending down and grasping her arm. "What's wrong? What happened?"

Kim kneeled down beside me. There was blood on my grandmother's forehead and on one of her ears. Her nightgown was wet; the glass on the night table had evidently broken and grape juice was seeping into the rug. "It's from the drink," Kim said. "I can smell it. It's that same grape stuff she brought in before. Where's she hurt?"

"Just on her back, I guess," I said. "She must have fallen again."

"What should we do?"

"I'll get a towel and wash it off. You stay with her."

I went to get a wet cloth while Kim began crawling around on the floor, picking up the pieces of glass that had splintered on the rug. When I returned, I began wiping her legs and arms, which were also stained with the sticky soda. Through her nightgown I could see her flat yellowish breasts and hard bulging belly, and I could smell the sweaty, unclean smell of her body. She sat quietly as I dried her. Then I covered her with one of my pajama tops with the sleeves rolled up. "There you are," I said, awkwardly, buttoning it. "Just the right size."

She looked at me dully and said nothing. She was no longer crying, but she still rubbed her back with her hand and moaned. "I could give her some more Valium," I whispered.

"What are you whispering for?" Kim said.

"I don't know," I said. "What do you think? Should I give her some more?"

Kim shrugged. "The other doesn't seem to have done her very much good."

"No, I guess not."

"Maybe she'd like something to eat," Kim said.

I leaned over and looked into my grandmother's face. "Do you want anything to eat, Granny?" I asked in a low voice.

"Euh! *Mein Gott!*" she murmured, still rocking back and forth. "*Mein Gott!*"

Together Kim and I got her up, holding her on each side. "Come on, here you go," I said. "Here you go!"

We lifted her up amidst groans and protests and carried her back to the bed. Once on it she lay flat on her back, blinking helplessly up at us like a turtle overturned on its shell. "Your mother will kill me," she murmured.

"Don't be silly," I said. "Mom doesn't care." I bent down and fumbled with the blanket, which was sliding off the bed. "You'll be fine in a little while, Granny. All will be well. Do not fear." That's what my father always used to say to me when I was little and had a bad dream.

19

By then it was getting late and Kim could see my mind wasn't ready to focus on calculus. "Want me to sleep over?" he asked.

"No, I'll be okay," I said, walking him to the door. "See you tomorrow."

After Kim left, I went right to bed. But I didn't fall asleep for a long time. For some reason I started remembering a time when I was around Kaylo's age and I woke up from a bad dream, hearing a rat gnawing inside the closet. I called my father, who staggered sleepily into my room, waited several moments, and then, hearing nothing, returned to bed. This happened three times and each time the steady gnawing of the rat disappeared as soon as my father appeared. "That's all right," my father said. "You're just a little worked up. Just go to sleep, okay?" But even the third time, after my father left, the sound began again. "Dad!" I called out, frightened at the sound of my own voice in the darkness. "Dad!" This time, as my father stood near the door, annoyed now and tired, there was silence. Then suddenly the gnawing began once more, louder this time, as though someone was knocking. "There!" I cried, sitting up in bed. "Yes," said my father. "Yes, I hear it." He began poking around in the closet while I lay in bed, trembling with nervous relief. "Yes, well, I can tell it's a rat," my father said finally. "We'll get it out in the morning, son." I wanted to ask if I could sleep in the chair in my parents' room, but I didn't. I lay in bed, silently, thinking of the rat, small and sleek and dusty with sharp teeth and a long thin tail, crouched in the closet, gnawing. "Charlie, Charlie, do not fear," my father said gently. "All will be well." And for several moments he stayed in my room to calm me, making patterns in the air with the burning red end of his cigarette.

CHAPTER THREE

Our first class Monday morning is presentation. Among ourselves we call it stage fright or just S.F. It's one of the classes that makes me wonder what I'm doing at Diamond. Actually, I had a choice of two schools for high school. I could have left Diamond (The Diamond School for the Arts) where I've been since first grade. To get into the high school you have to audition, just like the outsiders do. They don't automatically take you, even if you've been there all along. Actually I was kind of amazed I got in. They skipped me in second grade, which probably means my I.Q. peaked ten years ago. That's why I'm sixteen, a year younger than most of my class. This probably shows I'm not a true musician or maybe that I just don't care that much, but I wasn't that nervous when I auditioned. When I got home, my parents began manically asking me how I did and what it was like, and I told them I'd probably failed, just to needle them a little, but also because I thought I had. I'm not a musical whiz kid who's known, since he was three, that "Music Is Your Life," as Ms. Abbot, our theory teacher, is fond of saying. I'm not sure what my life is going to be, but I doubt it'll be anything that riveted. I'll be lucky to get a job.

All year kids give performances at the school assembly, which is held once a week. Presentation class is to discuss why some kids, who are really good at whatever they do, give rotten performances. It's to try and make you see that what Mr. Tuberosa calls "inner attitude" counts as much as practicing or knowing the music really well.

The kid who gave the performance sits in front of the class and Tuberosa asks him (or in this case her) how she thought it went. This particular Monday it was a dancer, Wendy Wolfe. Like most of the dancers, she's one of these almost anorexically thin types with waist-length black hair in a ponytail. She was in jeans and a white shirt and flat red shoes with a Band-aid on her shin.

"So, how did *you* think it went, Wendy?" Tuberosa said. Naturally the teachers are supposed to be impartial, but Tuberosa flirts with all of the even mildly pretty girls in a way that's kind of sickening. You couldn't nail him for sexual harassment. It's more subtle. He just kind of lowers his voice and questions them in a very tender, kindly voice, whereas with your average male, like me, he looks either bored or irritated.

Most dancers are pretty inarticulate. I guess that's why they become dancers. They're more body people than head people. Also, Wendy has a really quiet voice that you can hardly hear unless you're in the first row, which I was. "Well, I think — I don't know. I think it seemed okay. I mean, I didn't make

23

mistakes. But I — see, the pacing is supposed to build to a sort of crescendo? And I don't think it did. I think I started going too fast, just wanting it to be over."

Tuberosa looked at the rest of us. "Did any of you notice that?"

"Yeah, I noticed it," Pedro Martinez said. What does he know? He plays drums. "You rushed it. Your movements definitely lacked fluidity."

Here's this guy who's five feet four with hair all over his body and moves like an orangutan. What does he know about fluidity? But Tuberosa just turned to Wendy and said, "Were you conscious of it at the time?"

"A little. I just couldn't stop myself."

I could identify with that because somewhat the same thing happened when I had to sing *"Un'aura amorosa,"* an aria from *Così fan tutte* a month earlier. I'd worked with my voice coach on pacing for two months and then — I think this was partly because Mom took the morning off and sat in the front row — I just wanted to get the bloody thing over with. My voice coach, Ms. Haines, was pretty understanding. She says she should have been a psych major since most voice problems are personality related.

Before I knew what was happening I raised my hand and said, "I had that same problem last month when I sang. It's like you're half aware of it at the time and half not."

Basically I spoke up to make Wendy feel better. Tuberosa leaped on what I'd said. "It's 'like' you're half aware or simply you're half aware?" he said sarcastically. He hates anyone to use "like" in the middle of a sentence.

I turned red. "I was only half aware of it," I mumbled.

"Well, at least you were *half* aware of it," he said in the same voice. "We need to keep half the brain awake at all times." This was a dig at a time last month when I fell asleep in class. I tend to have insomnia fairly often and it got worse around January when my grandmother came to live with us. I'd be about to fall asleep and she'd appear in the doorway, scaring the bejeesus out of me.

"I think Wendy's piece was too much like the one she did last semester," Nadine Bem said. She's a stout girl with a beautiful soprano voice who I've occasionally thought likes me. It's not reciprocal. "I don't think she's trying to grow."

"What do you say to that, Wendy?" Tuberosa asked, his voice changing to that syrupy sweet tone again.

Wendy looked thoughtful. "I thought if I picked completely different music, it would — "

"But your movements were the same," Nadine put in.

"Nadine, let's let Wendy complete her thoughts, shall we?"

Wendy was twisting one leg around the other. "Yeah, I guess she's right," she said in a soft, hopeless voice.

"Well, *I* thought she was great," Selby Lile said loudly. "And I thought you were great the other time, too." Selby always feels he has to say something good to everyone. He had an uncle who com-

25

mitted suicide after a bad review, so he feels like he's personally protecting the egos of everyone in the class.

"Great isn't a very expressive adjective," Tuberosa said disdainfully, glancing at the wall clock. "Could you dilate on that slightly?"

"Wendy's so graceful," Selby said, completely unself-consciously. "And she has a beautiful body and she moves so gracefully. I wouldn't change a thing."

The class laughed. Wendy looked embarrassed.

All of a sudden something happened that is frequent with me lately. Wendy lost all of her clothes. It was like she was sitting there naked with nothing on but her flat red shoes and the Band-aid on her shin. I wonder how often this is supposed to happen when you're sixteen. I know it's not rare to think of sex, but I wonder about this particular phenomenon. The only person I've ever discussed it with is Kim and he's not, as it were, into girls yet. His parents are afraid that might distract him from his music, and probably they're right.

My parents are the opposite, or at least my father is. According to him, he was making it or almost making it with dozens of girls at my age. He thinks I'm socially backwards. When I was thirteen, he gave me this long talk on always using condoms and the dangers of VD. Then, when I turned fifteen, he brought up the subject again and asked how I was doing. When I said I wasn't doing anything, he looked horrified. "Why not? What's wrong?"

"Maybe I'm too fat," I said.

"Bull," he came back. "*I* was fat. Women don't

26

care. Women are a lot more thoughtful than men. They know what really counts is virility, and what does that have to do with size?" Search me. I'm not sure about where I stand virility-wise, either.

After presentation class I have calculus. I know Dad's motive in insisting I take it is that he doesn't want to be supporting me for the rest of his life and he thinks medicine is a good, secure profession. But what if I become a musical manager and plan other people's careers? That way I'd travel, but I'd also be more like an entrepreneur. I'd have a big office and delicate female musicians would sit nervously opposite me, hoping I would sign them up for a tour of China.

Mondays I pick Kaylo up on the third floor (which is where the fifth grade meets), and take him to his violin lesson. Then Josie, our housekeeper, gets him when the lesson's over. When I came to pick him up, he was dragging a gigantic papier mâché animal twice as big as he was behind him. "What the hell is that?" I asked.

"Guess," he said.

"A dragon?"

"Wrong." He looked gleeful.

"A dinosaur?" Kaylo knows more about dinosaurs than anyone outside the Smithsonian.

He looked scornful. "Yeah, but what kind?"

"A brontosaurus." I only remember that one and the mean one, the tyrannosaurus.

"There's no such *thing* as a brontosaurus," Kaylo said. "It's an apatosaurus. But you're wrong anyway."

"Okay, I give up."

"A polacanthus," Kaylo informed me. "Didn't you see the scales?"

"So, what are we supposed to do with it? It won't fit on the bus."

He lowered his voice. "I've saved money for a cab. You take it home and hide it in my closet. It's for Mom, for Mother's Day."

Great, just what she was hoping for: a polacanthus. "Why'd you make it so big?" I said.

"It's *not* big," he said impatiently. "It's not even life-size."

I looked at it. "Did they really have such little heads?"

"Of course." He looked important. "It's scientifically accurate, except for the colors."

Earlier in the year Kaylo was a superstar for the day. I remember that. When it happens, the class traces you on a big piece of brown paper, colors it in, and then makes a list of what they think of as your outstanding traits. Of Kaylo they said:

1. Kaylo is a very good piano player.
2. He has pretty hair.
3. He doesn't like to fight.
4. He knows a lot about dinosaurs.

We managed to get the dinosaur into a cab. I sat in front with the driver; Kaylo and the polacanthus got in back. Then I dropped Kaylo off at his lesson and took the cab the rest of the way home. I got into the elevator with our elevator man, Marcel, who said, looking at it, "Something from outer space?"

"A polacanthus," I said. "It's for Mother's Day."

He looked bewildered. He thinks Americans are crazy anyway.

Josie found me trying to stuff the polacanthus into Kaylo's closet. "What, may I ask, are you up to now?"

Josie and I have a playfully hostile relationship. She's black, thirty-seven, and divorced. No kids. She plays a mean game of poker and is under orders from her doctor to give up beer since he said her liver was enlarged. For some reason she dyes her hair red. I've seen pictures with it natural and it looks a lot better. I explained the situation.

Josie burst out laughing. "That's just what we need in this house. One more thing to keep clean. What'd *you* get her? The Eiffel Tower?"

"I forgot it was Mother's Day," I admitted sheepishly. "I'll think of something." It wasn't until Sunday.

"I am not lending you any money, boy. Don't even *ask* me."

"Who's asking?"

"You get an allowance. You save to buy your mama something elegant. Perfume. You do it *right*."

Josie's like my father. She thinks I'm hopeless with women. "I guess I ought to get Grandma something, too," I said, thinking aloud. I thought of the shell she and I had found together on the beach. "Where *is* she?"

Josie rolled her eyes. "The doctor has her out in the park — thank the good lord. You know what she did this morning? Said I stole her pearls. What pearls? She doesn't *have* any pearls! She *dreamed* about

29

pearls. So the doctor said, 'I'll get you some pearls, Mother.' Some pearls! He'll take her to the five-and-dime. She won't know the difference.''

Josie usually refers to my father, somewhat sarcastically, as "the doctor" and to my mother as "the madam." "So, listen, don't tell about the polacanthus till Sunday, okay?" I said.

"You haven't told me yet what you're going to get her."

"I haven't decided. . . . Perfume, maybe, like you said."

"What kind? There's thousands of perfumes. You want a hint?"

"Sure."

"Follow me."

I followed Josie into my parents' bedroom. She took a perfume bottle off my mother's dressing table and squirted it at me. "Get her a refill. Scoundrel Musk. It's rough stuff."

"How much does it cost? A hundred dollars a bottle?"

Josie laughed. "Boy, why are you so stingy? This is your *mother*."

"What are you getting *your* mother?" I countered.

"My mother doesn't need any perfume. She has men up to her eyeballs." Josie's mother is a sixty-year-old widow with a social life that sounds exhausting.

"So, how come *you* don't?" I said, just to needle her.

"Who *says* I don't?" Josie said. "Since when do you know the story of my life? And who's talking, huh? Who's so busy with the ladies himself?"

"I'm a late bloomer," I said, trying to smile at her ingratiatingly. It's important to stay on Josie's good side.

Josie just snorted.

CHAPTER FOUR

We eat late, at around eight. Dad gets home at seven and puts Granny to bed, a euphemism of sorts since frequently she's up within the hour. But sometimes she dozes off and we have a moderately peaceful meal. Josie is a great cook, which is probably the worst thing that could happen to our family. She's good at everything, even vegetables.

"I had a dream that a witch came into my room last night," Kaylo said. He mostly picks at his food since he has a sandwich at five.

Mom leaned forward. "What do you mean, a witch?"

"She had funny white hair and she stood near my bed and then she walked away."

Mom waited till Josie carted Kaylo off to bed, which she does just before we have dessert. Then she turned on my father. "Sam, really, this is impossible. You *know* that wasn't a witch. It was Gustel."

"I can't tie her into bed," my father said, sighing.

"Kaylo has always slept so well. Pretty soon he'll be like you and Charles, up half the night, asleep half the day."

Dad gave me a sly smile. "We're not *that* bad,

are we, Charles? I manage to stay awake at least four hours each day."

Mom looked at me. "How was it last night when we were out?"

I guess Dad hadn't told her about my phone call. "It was . . . okay," I said cautiously, for some reason shielding my father. "She wandered around a little. Then she settled down."

"Josie said there was glass on the carpet in her room and it looked like she'd spilled something."

"That was when she was taking her pills," I said. "She spilled some grape juice."

Mom sighed. "Sam, you know Josie was *not* hired as a nursemaid for an aging, cantankerous, paranoid old lady. She has enough to do looking after the house and Kaylo. What if she quits?"

"Then we'll kill ourselves," my father said. "A joint suicide."

"That's not funny," my mother said. "Josie has feelings. She said Gustel was accusing her of stealing!"

My father sighed. "I took care of that. I took her to the store and got her some fake pearls. Look, sweetie, this is a temporary situation. A solution will be found. She's my mother. She raised me, she gave me life. Be patient, okay?"

Mom got a wry expression. "Patience is not my forte."

"I'm aware of that," my father said dryly. "But I love you, I love her, I love Josie. I just want everyone to be happy."

Mom leaped up. "That's not possible! You're living in a dream world! Anyway, what does happiness mean to her? She doesn't know who anyone *is* half the time."

"She always knows who *I* am," Dad said. "Doesn't she know who you are?" he asked me.

"I *think* so," I said. Frankly, I'm not always sure.

"One of the tenets of marriage," Mom said, "is you choose your wife and children over your mother. I'm worried sick about what this will do to Kaylo. He's such a happy-go-lucky child. Now he's starting to have nightmares. He — "

"I *have* chosen you. . . . Enough, already! I'm exhausted. Where's dessert?"

My mother disappeared into the kitchen to get dessert.

My father stared gloomily at the ceiling. "Never have a mother," he said. "Never have a wife."

"How about a girl friend?" I asked.

He smiled. "You have a girl friend? Mazeltov! About time!"

"I don't have a girl friend," I said. "Relax."

Dad poured himself a third glass of wine. "It's those arty little girls at your school," he said. "They aren't the only fish in the sea. Don't be such a snob. There are plenty of perfectly lovely girls who work in dress shops, or in bakeries. There are lovely girls everywhere!"

I wished Mom would hurry up with dessert. "I know, Dad."

"So what's stopping you? Shyness? They don't care. They don't know. Pick some nice, lovely, lush, little — "

At that my mother entered the room with three

baba rhums on a platter. "You know, I can hear everything through the kitchen door," she said, shooting him a glance.

"I'm giving Charles advice," my father explained.

"Picking up strangers in the park? That's advice?"

"I didn't say he should pick up strangers."

"You want him to get VD? Charles is happy as he is, Sam! He is *normal*. Just because you were horny from the time you were in second grade, that doesn't mean all boys are, or should be."

My father looked abashed. "It's true. . . . I *was* horny. I spent all my time in class undressing all the girls, all the teachers even. . . . But I still got all A's."

I turned red, remembering the incident with Wendy. I'm afraid I'm just as horny as my father, I just don't do anything about it.

"Sam," my mother said, delving into her baba rhum. "Charles belongs to a new generation of men. Kind, thoughtful. They aren't out for what they can get. They want to give pleasure to the woman. They put that first."

Dad looked at me. "What self-restraint!"

"Charles probably has a perfectly fine, satisfactory sex life," Mom embroidered. "It's natural and normal that he doesn't talk about it to us."

My father was alternately eating his baba rhum and drinking more wine. "I would have been delighted if my father had been so understanding."

"No, you *wouldn't* have," Mom retorted. "You

loved thinking you were doing unspeakable things behind his back. That was the whole kick behind it.''

"Surely there was more to it than *that*," my father said. He raised his glass. "To Charles's sex life, whether it exists or not!"

I sighed. I'm not allowed to leave the table till everyone is finished.

As he reached for the bottle, my mother said, "You promised not to drink with dessert. You've *had* five glasses. Sam, please. You're going to die and leave us with your mother and I just plain don't have the energy to get involved with another man at my age."

My father put down the bottle. He kissed my mother. "I won't die," he said. "I promise."

Actually, my father has often said he won't live beyond sixty. He definitely looks older than fifty. He puffs when he runs and his skin is slightly gray.

It's funny about my parents. I'm probably one of the few kids in my class whose parents are still together, and even though I worry about everything from when I'll get a girl friend to nuclear war, I never worry about my parents splitting up. I guess it's that if you think of them as these paragons, these rare people who've managed to hack their way through twenty-five years together, you think of one of those TV families with a perky, ingratiating mother and a suavely forceful, successful father. Yeah, okay, I guess you could call my mother perky, though energetic might be more on target. And my father is successful in that he makes lots of dough.

But half their conversations or interactions are like the one that had just taken place at dinner, with both of them hurling insults and challenging remarks at each other. Maybe they like that. When I had a report to do for school, I asked each of them separately what they liked best about the other one. Dad said he liked Mom's iconoclasm and directness; Mom said she liked Dad's melancholy sense of hopelessness and weird sense of humor. Why should I argue with it? If they're happy, or what they define as happy, terrific.

It's not even that I have a burning desire to be part of what one might define as a normal family. First, I'm not sure that exists. And then there are probably as many variations on it as there are on horny sixteen-year-old guys. But when I visit Kim's family everything is so quiet and peaceful, and the idea of anyone getting into what in our family would be a routine family slugout, verbally, would be unheard of. Kim, of course, thinks my family is wonderfully dynamic and fascinating, and spends as much time here as he can.

After school the next day I went to a drugstore to buy some Scoundrel Musk for my mother for Mother's Day. It's not as original as a polacanthus, but it's something, and Josie ought to know what women like since she's one herself. I can't figure out why Josie doesn't have a boyfriend. Her husband, or ex-husband, Hobart, was a gorgeous black guy who bought a new Cadillac every year. When he pulled up stakes, she was kind of bitter and claimed she was "through with men." That was five years ago. I think she's still extremely attractive, though

I don't get why she dyes her hair red, especially when she keeps buying these cheapo wigs at Macy's to wear over her real hair.

I decided, instead of buying Mom one big bottle, to buy three little bottles — one for Mom, one for Josie, and one for Grandma. I figure Josie's never had a child and can't since she had a hysterectomy when she was twenty-five, so I'm about as close to a child of her own as she'll have. And I don't think she'd have recommended Scoundrel Musk if she didn't like it herself. As for Grandma, well, I hate saying this, but she smells so bad a lot of the time, this might help mask the smell.

Josie's right. I'm stingy. I get a pretty generous allowance, and Mom and Dad buy all my clothes and basic necessities. I buy the occasional record or book, but I'm not into drugs, which would be the main direction toward which my money could flow. At Diamond there are kids dealing everything after school — grass, cocaine. I've tried most of them at parties, but I figure I'm strange enough socially without having a drug habit as well.

Mother's Day was Sunday. When I got up at eight — I can't seem to sleep late, even on weekends — Dad was fixing Mom a special breakfast of waffles and sausages. Just the smell of everything made my stomach turn over the way your heart is supposed to turn over when someone you have a crush on passes by. I could see he'd made enough for all of us. Kaylo was "helping" him.

"Can I wake her up?" he kept asking excitedly.

"She'll be up soon," Dad said. "I have to deal with Grandma first."

Josie doesn't come in Sunday so Dad gives Grandma a kind of bath, more or less sponging her off, and gets her dressed. She has quite a few nice silk dresses from the time she and my grandfather lived in Florida. I stole a sausage while this was going on and then all of us, including my grandmother, trooped into Mom and Dad's bedroom.

Mom was up already, reading in bed, and had the good grace to look surprised and delighted. She hugged Dad, and said, the way she always does, "Let's eat in the dining room. I think it's easier."

While we were eating, Kaylo, who'd finished first, as always, dragged in his polacanthus. He "presented" it to Mom with a proud expression on his face. She looked disconcerted just for a moment and then said, "Why, that's lovely, Kaylo. It's a dinosaur, isn't it?"

"Yeah, but what kind?"

Needless to say, no one in the family is up on dinosaurs, but since Mom reads to Kaylo a lot, she guessed, "A pterodactyl?"

He looked at her like she was crazy. "It doesn't have wings!"

"That's true, it doesn't. Let's see — a tyrannosaurus?"

"Wrong!" he shouted gleefully. To Dad he said, "*You* guess."

"A polacanthus?" Dad guessed.

Kaylo looked angry, and scowled. "How did you know?"

"Just a lucky guess," Dad said, adding heavy cream to his coffee.

My grandmother was stuffing in a big helping of waffles and sausages. "*I* want to guess," she said.

That was a little redundant since the right answer had just been given, but my father said, "What do you guess, Granny?"

She thought a minute, and then said with a sly smile, "A monster."

"You're right," my father said. "It *does* look a little like a monster."

Kaylo darted over to my grandmother's side. "It's for Mother's Day," he said, "and this is for you because you were a mother once, too."

"I'm still a mother," my grandmother said, beaming proudly at my father. "I have the finest son in the world." To Kaylo and me she said solemnly, "Your father is the most wonderful man in the world. And the most brilliant. And the most kind."

This is the kind of thing that makes smoke start coming out of Mom's ears, but Kaylo just said impatiently, "Aren't you going to open your present?"

He'd made her "A Book of Dinosaurs," hand-drawn with a few sentences describing each one. My grandmother hugged him. "You're a darling," she said.

Ultimately, seeing Kaylo hog every family occasion gets on my nerves, though I realize I should be understanding since he's only ten. I brought out the two small bottles of Scoundrel Musk and gave one to Mom and one to my grandmother.

My mother looked delighted. "Why, how thoughtful, Charles! I was just running out. And that's my favorite perfume. How did you guess?"

I just looked sheepish; I figured Josie would forgive me if I didn't tell.

My grandmother was just looking at the present. She hadn't even opened it. "Here, let me help you," Dad said, and then added, "Wow! You two ladies are going to set every man within firing range on his ear." Playfully he squirted a little at my grandmother.

"It's too strong," she said, suddenly irritable. "It'll make me smell like a whore. Like that shvartza who comes in every day."

I guess that means Josie. It's a Yiddish expression for a black woman. "Oh Christ," my mother said, rolling her eyes. "I can't take this again."

I must admit I felt a little hurt. Maybe it *was* a dumb present for an eighty-two-year-old lady. "Sorry," I said, picking up the wrapping paper.

"What's a whore?" said Kaylo, who picks up on everything.

"It's a woman who likes to appeal to men," my father said quickly. Suddenly he jumped up. "Look at this beautiful day. Let's go for a picnic!"

"Yay! Great!" Kaylo said.

My mother was clearing the table. "Portia and I have to plan that party for next week," she said, "but you all go. . . . And thanks so much, everyone, for the presents." Dad had gotten her a pink blouse, which she was wearing.

I can always sense my mother's tension when my grandmother is around. I guess she feels she can't say anything so she just gets tight-lipped and crisp and finds some excuse to clear out. Before my grandmother lived with us, it wasn't like this. I hope it doesn't last forever.

CHAPTER FIVE

My father, Kaylo, my grandmother, and I all went out to the park. On the way my father stopped at the local deli, Martin's, for some supplies. "Pickles!" Kaylo yelled. "Get lots of pickles!"

My father always gets lots of pickles because he loves them himself. In fact, he loves everything he's not supposed to eat, like smoked salmon, cream cheese, heavy cream in his coffee. He says he's a Sybarite.

It's funny the way my grandmother's moods change. One minute you look at her and she seems like a regular little old lady, making charming, slightly disconnected remarks, and then she'll say something really rude and out of place like calling Josie a whore. I know she can't help it. It's just Alzheimer's, a disease where certain brain cells disintegrate, but there are times when I can understand Mom getting so annoyed with her. Kaylo has moods, too, and says rude things, but he's never really cruel.

Dad led us up to Eightieth and Fifth, behind the Metropolitan Museum, and found a nice place under a tree. It was cool and mildly sunny, a nice day for a picnic. Then he took out all the food: sandwiches, beer, pound cake, chocolate bars.

"But Samuel, we just ate!" my grandmother exclaimed.

"Just a little snack," my father said. "No one has to eat if they're not hungry."

Kaylo, of course, can eat nonstop all day and never gain a pound. I was never like that, even when I was growing six inches a year. I just figured I was allowed to eat that much more and did. But I tried to stick to just a bagel with some butter, and a beer. Kaylo ate a few pickles and then began running around picking dandelions for my grandmother. As we were sitting there, I looked up and my heart sank. There was Wendy Wolfe from my presentation class with what looked like her parents. She was dressed in a real dress, her father was in a suit, and her mother was slim and dark-haired with a big floppy hat. I promised God anything She wanted (Josie's convinced me God is a black woman), if She would let Wendy not see me. I looked off to one side so I couldn't catch her eye, but then couldn't resist darting a glance back to see if they were out of sight. Just then Wendy saw me. "Oh hi, Charles," she said in a friendly way. She and her parents came over to where we were sitting on the grass. "These are my parents. Charles is in my class at Diamond."

"Well, I'm glad to see it really is a coed school," her father said. "Sometimes I wonder."

It's always a relief when other people's parents make dumb, embarrassing remarks. Feeling much better, I said, "This is my father and my grandmother, and my brother Kaylo."

Kaylo ran over and said, "We're celebrating

Mother's Day." He handed Wendy a bunch of dandelions.

"I'm not a mother," she said, blushing.

Kaylo looked at Wendy's mother. "Are *you* a mother?"

"Yes, I am," she said.

"You take them, then."

Then my father made the remark I was hoping against hope he wouldn't make. "Would you fine people like to join us in a little snack? I'm afraid we brought more for our picnic than we should have."

Say no, please.

"Why, we were just about to look for a place to have some lunch," Mrs. Wolfe said. "That would be lovely, if you're sure you have enough."

My father stood and with a gracious gesture said, "We'd be honored."

Why am I such a slob? It's true I didn't expect to run into anyone from our school, especially a girl, but I was wearing old filthy jeans and a wrinkled shirt. I looked like a bum. Some guys can dress like that and look macho, as though they just didn't care much about clothes (because they look so great without them), but not me. Why couldn't we have left my grandmother at home? She's going to do something mortifying and Wendy'll hate me forever.

Mr. Wolfe sat down next to my father. "I'm a stockbroker," he said. "James Wolfe."

My father shook his hand with that mocking gallantry he has. "Sam Goldberg, pathologist." My mother has trained him to always ask people's wives what they do, but Mrs. Wolfe said, before he could even ask, "I'm Cindy Wolfe and I don't work. Sometimes I feel like a dinosaur."

That got Kaylo's attention. "What kind?" he asked.

"Kaylo is our in-house dinosaur expert," Dad said.

Mrs. Wolfe smiled. She was really pretty. "I just meant I feel I belong to a species that's becoming extinct."

"You beautify the earth," my father said. "What more valuable function can any being perform?" Maybe if you're fat like my father, you learn to develop a line with women. I should work on that.

"What's *your* line, Charles?" Mr. Wolfe asked. "You're not a dancer, I hope?"

Need he have asked? "I play the piano and I sing."

"Charles has a great voice," Wendy said. "He sang in assembly last month."

"Let's hear a few bars," Mr. Wolfe said.

I tried quickly to think if there was any situation in the world that could be more embarrassing than this and decided there wasn't. At least it would be a distraction from my grandmother doing something crazy. I allowed a minute or two for the earth to open up under me. Then I just sang *"Un'aura amorosa."* When I was done, they all clapped. My grandmother hugged me. "He's *such* a fine boy!" she said. "Like his father."

"Only I can't sing," my father said.

"Is that how you're going to earn a living?" Mr. Wolfe asked me keenly, opening a container of Greek olives.

46

"He's considering medicine," my father answered for me.

"That's the stuff," Mr. Wolfe said, wolfing down a bunch of olives. "Earn a decent living. Sing on the side. That's what I tell Wendy. Dance in the living room! Learn how to type! Get an MBA!"

Wendy really looked annoyed. "Daddy, I'm not going to dance in the living room! I may not rise to the top of my profession, but I'm certainly not going to get an MBA or something ridiculous like that." Suddenly she smiled shyly. "And I'm not going to get up and dance right here. I'm not as confident as Charles."

"We can see you'd be a wonderful dancer," my father said. "Even without seeing you."

"*I'm* a wonderful dancer," Kaylo said. And without any coaxing, he began doing some kind of very peculiar dance on the lawn.

"A very talented family," Mrs. Wolfe said. "My husband tends to forget that the arts are a profession, just as medicine or — what was it you did?" she asked my father.

"I'm a pathologist," Dad said.

"I'm not absolutely sure what that is," Mrs. Wolfe said, smiling.

"Many days I'm not, either," my father said. He glanced nervously over at my grandmother. "How're you doing, Granny?" What he meant was did she need to go to the bathroom. Sometimes she forgets and then pees on the floor. *Please don't let her do that now. Triple please.*

"How should I be?" my grandmother said. "I'm fine."

47

"Why don't we make a little trip into the museum," my father said. "You come, too, Kaylo."

"I don't need to go," Kaylo said, pouting.

"You just come for the ride," my father said. He helped my grandmother to her feet. As she stood up, a trickle of urine came down both legs. "I guess we're a little late. . . . Well, let's go anyway."

My grandmother looked down at the pool beneath her and said, with a shrug, to the Wolfes, "I'm not what I once was."

I'd been hoping after my father, Kaylo, and my grandmother disappeared, the Wolfes would say they needed to go, too. I felt so awful about the whole incident, so ashamed, I just wanted to disappear. Who invented families? Why do they wreck things just when you need them most?

Mrs. Wolfe just sipped her coffee and said, "Is she in a home?"

"No, she lives with us," I explained.

"We tried that with my mother, but it wrought havoc on the family," she said.

"But our grandmother was crazy," Wendy said. "She had Alzheimer's. Yours doesn't seem to be like that."

"She is a lot of the time," I said. God, Wendy looked pretty. Her collar bones jut out and her breasts are small, but she has beautiful big dark eyes with long eyelashes. She ought to wear her hair loose all the time, instead of tied back that way.

Finally Wendy's father staggered to his feet. "I think we better be heading along," he said. "This has been a very pleasant interlude, Charles. Tell your father we enjoyed meeting him."

"Your little brother is darling," Wendy said.

How about me? Aren't *I* darling?

After the Wolfes had departed, I sat on the grass, gazing dreamily off into the distance. Now that the occasion was over, I reviewed it and touched it up a little. Look on the bright side, right? Gaze at the doughnut, not at the hole. Okay, the doughnut. First, I do have a good singing voice, much deeper and more self-assured and "masculine" than my speaking voice. I was asked to sing and I sang. They thought I was good, maybe not "great" as Wendy overgenerously suggested, but I didn't flub the occasion, my voice didn't crack. And Mr. Wolfe even saw me as someone who could, if he wanted, become a doctor. . . . Let's see, what else? Well, Wendy was definitely friendly. She, too, once had a crazy grandmother, so maybe mine didn't seem so weird. My father can strike people as charming and they only stayed around for about twenty minutes. Plus, he must have seemed generous, offering food and drink to total strangers. And Kaylo, though he can be a show-off and a pest, is also what most people consider "cute" for his age.

I let all this roll over me until I saw the three of them trooping back, my father looking harassed and sweaty. "They wouldn't let me in the ladies' room. She peed all over the lobby."

It was all over, but I still felt rotten. My father takes my grandmother places as though she was the way she used to be ten years ago. Then we had lots of terrific picnics in the park. Can't he see how everything is different now?

"Did she do it on a Rembrandt?" I said.

49

"Get everything together," my father said, ignoring this. "I'm taking her home. Kaylo, you want to stay with Charles and help him or go home with Grandma and me?"

"Stay with Charles," Kaylo said promptly.

Kaylo helped me put the rest of the food in the shopping bag. "Where's the girl and the lady and the man?" he asked.

"They had to go." My good mood was oozing irretrievably away.

"Is she your girl friend?" Kaylo asked.

"Which one?"

He roared with laughter. "The pretty one!"

"They were both pretty." Why do I enjoy needling Kaylo so much?

"The young one!" he yelled with exasperation at my seeming denseness.

"Not really," I admitted, swallowing the rest of the beer.

"How come?"

I made a mock demure expression. "I'm shy."

Kaylo laughed again. "You are not!"

"I'm not sure she likes me," I admitted. And I couldn't think of any good reason why she should.

"She likes *me*," Kaylo said. "Maybe she'll be *my* girl friend."

It's true, she'd said he was darling. "Will you invite me to the wedding?" I said. "I can be your best man."

"What's best man?" said Kaylo, grabbing a few Oreos before I got the package away from him.

"It's the best man you know . . . which I am."

50

He gave me a disdainful look. "You're not a man! You're a boy. Daddy's a man."

"I am so a man," I said in an unnaturally deep voice.

That started Kaylo rolling on the grass, laughing again. "That was so funny when you sang," he said. "You looked so funny!"

"How do you think you looked dancing?"

We finally got all the stuff together and walked home slowly. Kaylo insisted on carrying one of the shopping bags, though he tilted dangerously to one side, as though he were drunk. Sometimes I envy Kaylo, being young enough not to have to care about girls or whether they like him, about anything that matters. He's lucky and he doesn't even know it.

CHAPTER SIX

Monday afternoon, when I got home from school, I gave Josie the bottle of Scoundrel Musk. She was in the kitchen slicing up apples for an apple pie. There's no way to describe Josie's apple pie. Think of the best apple pie you've ever had or ever hope to have and then multiply that by a thousand. She never uses a recipe, just tosses everything in. I've tried watching her and even making one myself, but it never came out the same.

I set the gift-wrapped package down on the table in front of her.

She looked up suspiciously. "What's *that* supposed to be?"

I smiled. "Happy Mother's Day."

"I ain't no mother, Charles, and I never have been, and unless there's some kind of miracle birth, I never will be."

"Well, I figured I was as close to a child as you'd get, so. . . ."

She gave me an affectionately scornful glance. "And you ain't no child, either. You're a man."

I felt flattered. "Look, will you open it? I spent my hard-earned money."

Josie snorted. "Hard-earned! Huh!" But she opened

it. She frowned. "I thought I told you to get that for your mama."

"I did. . . . I got one for her and you and Grandma."

Josie turned the bottle around in her hand. "Well, that was a nice gesture, Charles." She smiled mischievously. "And, boy, it may come in handy sooner than you think."

"How come?" I pulled up a chair to sit and watch her slicing apples.

"Well, you know Willie, the doorman who comes on in the back at eight?"

"Sure." Willie is a short, stout, balding man with eyes of two different colors. My father claims he's a great untapped scholar and is always having long conversations with him about Carlos Castenada and Martin Buber.

"He asked me out. . . . What do you think of that?"

"But he's Jewish!"

Josie raised her eyebrows. "So? I'm not prejudiced. I thought they were supposed to be the chosen people or some such thing."

"And he's old! He must be a lot older than you." Somehow the idea disgusted me. Willie to me was a grubby old man.

"He's fifty-two, his wife died, he's lonely, we're both hard up. . . . Why shouldn't I give him a chance? They say he's rich."

There's a rumor that, even though Willie lives in one room in the back of the building, he's salted away millions. Somehow I doubt it. "Bullshit. You can do better than that."

"I can? Where? Show me." Josie reached over

and grabbed my arm. "You know something, Mr. Charles A. Goldberg? One reason *you* don't have nobody, despite your age and wherewithal, is you are too damn fussy. *You* look for faults. Where's *that* going to get you?"

This is true.

"Now, I want you to help me with a crucial decision," Josie said. "You wait here, okay?"

"Sure." I sat patiently, waiting, for a couple of minutes. Josie came back with two wigs, one dark brown curls, one a kind of blond Afro. "Now, one of these can be returned to the store and my question is, which one?"

"You can't return both?"

"Charles, what was I just saying about your character? Now if you listened to me once in a while, you'd have something to do in the evenings yourself other than baby-sit your little brother." She pulled on the dark brown wig. "Okay, regard!"

I regarded.

Then she pulled it off and put on the blond wig.

I regarded some more.

Josie put the second wig back in the bag. "So, which do you prefer? I want a man's opinion. The honest, unvarnished truth."

Even *I* know enough about women never to give them that. "I kind of like your natural hair," I said, "if you wouldn't dye it red."

Josie looked horrified. "What hair? I don't *have* any hair! Why do you think I wear this wig?"

"It's just that if you wear a wig all the time, your real hair gets all flattened out. Why don't you try and be natural?"

"Charles, I am at an age when natural is shit. If I was natural, I'd be gray, boy. I'd look like an old lady."

"No, you wouldn't," I said. "Your skin isn't at all wrinkled or anything."

Josie beamed. "You're right. I've got good skin. That's from mama."

"So, why dye it red? Anyone can tell it's not real."

"I like red hair. I see myself as the red-haired type. Fiery tempered, feisty. . . ."

"Yeah, I can see that," I said dryly.

Josie socked me. "Do you want to know one basic difference between me and you?"

"Sure, sock it to me . . . only not literally, or I'll be black and blue and they'll haul you off for child abuse."

"*I* give life a chance and *you* just sit around and criticize. Now you could ask why, because here *I* am black, poor, my husband ran off, and *you* are white, rich, and could have any girl friend you set your mind to having. But what I have that you lack is character."

I sighed. "Yeah, you're right."

Josie said, "But Charles, what are you going to do about it? That's what I'm asking. You just sit around in your room waiting for the world to end. No girl's going to walk into your room! You have to make yourself available, be charming."

"Josie, listen, I appreciate all this well-intentioned advice, but one, I'm not charming, I have lousy skin, I'm fat. . . ."

She shook her head. "That is all self-pity, and

55

that is *all* it is. Look at my mother. She's twice your size and twice your age and she has men lined up outside the door. Men of all ages!"

Just then my grandmother walked into the room. She walks so quietly that I wasn't aware she was there until she was right behind me. "Hi, Granny," I said.

She ignored me and pounced on the perfume, which Josie had left on the marble table. "Mine!" she said angrily.

"No, hey, wait a sec," I said. "That's Josie's. I gave you one like it. This one belongs to Josie."

"Thief!" my grandmother said to Josie. She turned and wheeled out of the room, taking the perfume with her.

I leaped to my feet.

"Let her be," Josie said wearily, though clearly disgusted. "She's old."

"No, I won't." I followed my grandmother down the hall and into her room. "Granny, that's Josie's perfume. I bought it for her for Mother's Day. Let's find your perfume, the one I got you." I looked around the room. My grandmother's room is such a mess, it's hard to find anything. "Where did you put it?"

My grandmother pointed to the bureau.

"Okay, well, what happened to it?"

"The shvartza stole it."

I felt really mad. "Granny, listen, first of all, Josie isn't a thief, okay? She's never stolen anything in her life. I gave her that perfume ten minutes ago. . . . And also it's rude to call someone a shvartza.

56

It's not a nice expression. Who cares if she's Jewish? Who cares if anyone is Jewish?"

My grandmother was looking at me as though I was crazy. Part of me was so mad that I wanted to snatch the perfume away from her, but she had it clutched tightly in her hand. Then she put it in her pocket. I reached over and tried putting my hand in her pocket. "Let me just see it, okay?"

"Thief!" my grandmother screamed, backing away.

Just then my father walked in. "What's going on here?"

"Thief, thief!" My grandmother ran to my father and clung to him as though I was some unknown assailant who had broken unexpectedly into her room.

"She took the perfume I bought Josie for Mother's Day. It's not fair," I said breathlessly. "*She's* the thief."

"Charles, this is absurd. Grandma wouldn't steal anything."

"Dad, I was right in the room. I saw her. She just grabbed it. She took Josie's perfume."

My grandmother was whimpering and clutching my father as though I might physically attack her. "Okay, Granny, let's calm down," my father said. "Let's see that nice perfume Charles got you for Mother's Day."

My grandmother took it out of her pocket and gave it to my father.

My father looked puzzled. "This is the perfume you gave your mother."

I sighed. "Dad, listen. I got three bottles of perfume, identical, for Mother's Day, one for Mom, one for Josie, one for Grandma. So obviously she thinks the one I gave Josie is hers and hers is probably lost."

"Then get the one you gave your mother and give it to Josie." My father sighed.

I went into my mother's bedroom. Her perfume was sitting on the bureau. I brought it in to Josie, not explaining. "Happy Mother's Day," I said, smiling ironically.

"What'd you do? Arm wrestle her to the ground?"

"Dad came home. . . . God, women are complicated! And you want me to have a girl friend, too?"

"Yes, I do," Josie said. She turned the oven on and patted the crust around her pie. "And I want you to bring her to this house so I can get a look at her and I want you to invite me to the wedding and I want to see a photo of your first child. That's all I ask. Then I'll sit back and rest peacefully."

"I hope you're not going to sit on the edge of your seat till all this happens," I said.

"I sure am. That's just where I'm going to sit." Josie gave me a smug glance.

In a way I must admit I feel flattered that Josie thinks someone could like me. Of course, what does she know? Anyone who'd go out with Willie doesn't have such great judgment, but she's right about everything else. I am too critical, I am too passive.

When I passed by Dad's study, he was sitting in

his chair, reading. "She's asleep. We'll figure it out later."

I hesitated. "Dad, what'd you think of that girl, the one we ran into over the weekend, the one from my class?"

"Too skinny," he said dismissively, not even looking up from his book.

"Did you think she was pretty?"

"What?"

This was useless. "Did you think the girl was pretty?"

Finally my father put his book down. "Charles, what you need is someone a little earthy, a little warm, even a little zaftig, maybe. You're too cerebral, you're too — Maybe even someone with a little experience? After that, you can go after one of those arty ones."

I left the room. I hate my father. I hate Josie. I hate myself. Are my faults that obvious that everyone in the family has to give me advice all the time? And I hate girls like the ones my father described, not that they're exactly throwing themselves at me. There's a girl like that in my singing class — Theresa Byers — who's chubby with big boobs and a booming laugh and what might be called a "bad rep." My father would love her. I should get them together.

CHAPTER SEVEN

The next day, spurred on by Josie's advice, I asked Wendy out.

"I thought maybe if you weren't busy next Saturday, we might take in a show or a concert?" Take in? Meaning imbibe?

"Do you have tickets?"

"No, but I could get some, if you're free."

For a scarily long moment Wendy hesitated. "I'd love to, Charles. Why don't we look at the paper during lunch and see what's playing?"

Success! But in the next period, which Wendy isn't in, I started wondering: What's wrong with her? Why is she so hard up that she said yes so fast? Doesn't she have any standards? Am I the first person to ask her out? My father thinks she's anorexic. Her arms *are* kind of weedy. . . . Stop! This is what Josie said you do too much of. She's right. Doughnut, not hole. Doughnut, doughnut!

At lunch we looked at *The New Yorker* and found a Neil Simon play, *Biloxi Blues*, that Wendy said she'd heard was good. I said I'd call about tickets. "Is your grandmother all right?" she asked.

What grandmother? Oh, right. "Well, she's pretty much the same. It's an ongoing condition. No cure. It can only get worse." Doughnut!

"She seemed sweet," Wendy said, opening her honey and pear yogurt. I gathered that was her entire lunch.

Somehow "sweet" isn't how I think of my grandmother after the incident with Josie's perfume. "It's kind of hard on everyone," I said. "She wanders around at night, she doesn't always know where she is."

Wendy started delicately spooning up her yogurt. I have to remember never to consume food in front of her; she'd probably faint with disgust. "It happened to my grandmother after my grandfather died," she said. "Everyone thought it would be a relief for her, in a way, when he died, she was getting so exhausted taking care of him because he had Parkinson's disease. But I guess looking after him gave her something to do."

"That's a little like what happened with mine," I said. "My grandmother used to take my grandfather to Florida every winter before they moved down there. She was a masseuse, I mean she gave massages to people." You have to be careful to put that the right way because otherwise it sounds like my grandmother worked in a massage parlor. "She gave massages to ladies, I guess to make them relax or cure their migraines or something."

"So, at least she had a profession," Wendy said. "I think that's important. All *my* mother does is shop and have lunch with her friends."

I remembered our picnic. "Your mother's really pretty, though."

"So?" Wendy had finished her yogurt and angrily

61

clamped the top onto the container. "There's more to life than being pretty!"

I laughed nervously. "I wouldn't know." To get her less angry I said, "She's not as pretty as you, though."

Wendy looked embarrassed. "But I'm more than pretty," she said. Then she turned red. "I mean, that's not the main thing about me."

Maybe to her it isn't. No, I'm not saying that's the only reason I'm asking Wendy out, but on the other hand it isn't completely irrelevant. I guess I don't have the art of giving women compliments. I have to ask Josie about it.

After school I called the theater and they said they had two tickets for this Saturday's performance. I decided to get orchestra seats. Why not go the whole hog? As I was stepping out of the phone booth, Kim said, "There you are. I was looking for you."

Mondays Kim usually has violin lessons. "I thought you had violin."

"I do. . . . I just wanted to ask if you were free Saturday. I have two tickets for Zuckerman."

I sucked in my breath, "God, I'm really sorry, Kim. The thing is, my parents got these tickets for *Biloxi Blues*, and I told them I'd go with them. I'd a lot rather have gone with you to hear Zuckerman."

"Another time," he said. "Well, see you tomorrow."

What's wrong with me? Lying to my best friend? Why shouldn't I be proud that I asked Wendy out and that she said yes? Is it because Kim doesn't go out with girls yet and I'm afraid he'll regard me as a traitor? No, that's not his personality. He'd probably just be admiring. Is it because I regard *myself* as a traitor? Partly, but a traitor to what? I'm not one of these guys who's hung up on male bonding. In fact, I frankly haven't seen a whole lot of it in my meager sixteen years on this earth. I think it's that I'm afraid the date with Wendy may be an unbelievable disaster. If it is, I don't want anyone, even Josie or my parents, to know it took place. I'm going to lie to everyone. Hung for a lamb, hung for a sheep. Or is it the other way around?

Saturday afternoon I told my parents I was going to a Zuckerman concert with Kim and couldn't baby-sit for Kaylo. "You could have told us a little earlier," my mother said, looking annoyed.

"Yeah, sorry, I forgot." They were leaving for dinner before I'd have to leave to pick Wendy up and I hoped to return before they did so there wouldn't be any suspicious remarks about my wearing my best suit. I expected Josie would leave at six, the way she usually does Saturday, but when I went into the kitchen for a quick snack to calm my nerves, she was sitting there, reading the *Daily News*. She looked at me and whistled.

"I'm just going to a concert with Kim," I said, opening the refrigerator door. "Relax."

"Yeah? So what's that 'Date with Wendy' on your planning board? Did Kim have some sex change operation or something?"

"You're a real sneak," I said. I found an old lamb chop that looked half eaten. I bit into it halfheartedly. "Who said you could look at my planning board?"

63

"Boy, one of my jobs in this house is to dust *all* surfaces. And one surface is your planning board and God gave me eyes to see what lies in front of me. I'm delighted. It's about time."

"Don't be too delighted till it's over," I said gloomily. "It'll probably be a disaster."

"Charles, now what did you promise me?"

"I didn't promise you anything."

"You promised me you were going to work on your attitude."

"Okay, it's going to be a swell date and Wendy is a swell girl and we're going to a swell play. Satisfied?"

Josie shook her head. "It's your life."

"Really? I thought it was somebody else's. I thought they got it mixed up. How come you're wearing that wig? I thought you were going to go natural."

Josie looked really fed up. She set down her newspaper, or can you call the *News* a newspaper? She set down her tabloid and said, "I'm aiming for glamorous, not natural. His first wife was a blonde so I figure he likes blondes."

"Whose first wife?"

"Willie! Charles, don't you listen to anything I say?"

"So that's why you're here late? Willie? He's a dirty old man."

"Well, *I* intend to give him a chance. And I advise you to do the same with that Miss Wendy whom you are gracing with your gracious company."

"I'll try."

Frankly, I think Josie looks like a hooker when

64

she wears those wigs. Still, passing a mirror, I thought: At least people pay hookers for their company. No one would pay me, even in my best suit. Boy, I hope running into Josie before my date won't jinx it. I hate the way she knows everything that's going on in my life. Most guys just have to deal with their mothers.

As I was leaving the apartment, I ran into a teenage girl who almost bumped into me. She was potentially pretty, but had braces and hair that stood up on end in a punky way. "Is this the Goldberg apartment?" she asked.

I figured she was the baby-sitter. "Yeah, good luck."

I'd arranged to meet Wendy in front of the theater. She was there before me, wearing a full-skirted red dress and those flat ballet-type shoes she usually has on at school. "There were certain complications at our house," I said. "Sorry I'm a little late." It's amazing how almost every word out of my mouth is a lie. I've just begun noticing it.

"Oh, you're not late," Wendy said. "I'm early. I always am. When I try to come late, I arrive on time."

Our seats were in the first row of the orchestra. The play was fair, but there were a number of auxiliary problems. One, the air conditioning was viciously strong and Wendy hadn't brought a sweater. In a movie, that would've been a perfect opportunity to put my arm around her to warm her up, as it were, but in plays, especially in the orchestra, people don't make out. So she sat there shivering and blowing her nose and I felt like a fool for not having taken her to a movie. Now she'll come down with bronchitis and never forgive me. "It's my fault," she said. "I should have remembered how they air-condition theaters."

The other thing I hate with plays — maybe this is more true with Neil Simon since people expect him to be funny and they've paid a lot for their seats — but everyone was *screaming* with laughter at everything, even the things that weren't funny. It was worse than a laugh track on TV. So even the things that were funny, you'd start to laugh and then you'd look next to you and see some idiot doubled over with laughter and you'd stop right in the middle. By the last act nothing even struck me as funny anymore.

Wendy and I went to Sardi's afterward. I ordered Irish coffee and cheesecake and she ordered tea and a fresh fruit cup. "So, how'd you like it?" I said. I was trying to remember Josie's advice about not being overly critical. I figured if Wendy liked it, I'd say I liked it, too.

"Well, I hate plays where the only women characters are a good-natured prostitute and a sweet, innocent Catholic girl whose whole function is to admire the hero."

Sometimes I wonder if girls like that exist. Maybe Neil Simon makes them up because they never did exist in real life. Probably he just went out with incredibly bright, sarcastic Jewish girls and he's never recovered. "Well, I hate plays where all the Jewish guys are either thin, intense, screwed-up intellectuals, or sweet would-be writers who're going to end up being multimillionaires."

Wendy nodded solemnly. "I guess one should never see a play that gets good reviews. They're always lousy."

Boy, did I wish Josie were here! She thinks *I'm* critical. Actually, I agreed. They brought our desserts. "You don't eat that much," I observed.

I thought that was an innocuous kind of remark, but Wendy said, "And you eat too much! So?"

Okay, that's it. From now on I'm going to hang around outside Marymount and find a girl with a big gold cross around her neck and gigantic boobs. I turned away, wounded to the core.

Wendy touched my arm gently. "I'm sorry, Charles. It's just, I thought you would know it's something I'm sensitive about. This may seem strange, but it's a big effort for me to eat in front of people, even now."

She sounded genuinely contrite so I said, "Why?"

Wendy looked puzzled. "Do you really not know?"

"Uh uh."

"I was anorexic last year. I was out of school for four months. They had me hospitalized. I went down to eighty-five pounds."

"No, I guess I didn't. I really didn't."

She laughed bitterly. "You think everyone will notice, but probably everyone is just absorbed in their own problems."

True. "That must have been rough," I said. The Irish coffee looked so good I decided to dive in, despite the conversation.

"I suppose it seems like a cliché," Wendy said. "The shy, anorexic girl, parental pressure, has to do everything perfectly. But everyone is different! I'm *not* a cliché!"

"I didn't think you were," I said sincerely. "What, um, causes that? Anorexia? I really don't know much about it."

"Well, I used to look just like you," Wendy said, spooning up a grape. "I was fat, sloppy, my parents were always screaming at me about the way I dressed. And then one day I looked in the mirror and felt such a wave of disgust! I was determined I would at least lose weight, even if I'd never have boys asking me out. Not that I wanted that."

Boy, she really has the art of making a guy feel wonderful: "just like you: fat, sloppy." If I had any sense, I'd walk right out and leave her to pay the bill herself. Here I paid seventy dollars for the tickets, this'll come to about ten or fifteen dollars, for what? Just to get insulted by some former anorexic who's never been on a real date? Wendy was looking at me. "I'm sorry, Charles. I didn't realize how sensitive you were. You seem very honest. I just wanted you to know . . . I know how you feel."

"How do you know?" I muttered, savagely attacking the cheesecake. "You're *not* me! Maybe I don't consider myself fat *or* sloppy. Maybe I think I'm God's gift to the opposite sex."

"Well, I didn't," Wendy said. "I just went around feeling ashamed and terrible all the time. I thought maybe that was how you felt, or why would you have asked me out?"

"I asked you out because my father thinks I'm a social failure who doesn't know anything about girls." Since she thought I was honest, I figured I might as well be.

"Well, *I'm* a social failure who doesn't know anything about boys," Wendy said, and giggled. "So, I guess we're well-matched. Actually, boys scare me, or men, I should say."

"What's so scary about them — or rather us?" I have to remember I'm part of the pack.

"Well, it's not so much boys your age, but more the way when they grow up, they either become like Tuberosa, always acting condescending and cheap, or like my father, always putting women down, or like all those guys you read about in the paper who push women in front of subway trains and then get a weekend in jail on an insanity plea."

There was a moment of silence.

"I never pushed anyone in front of a subway train," I said.

"I don't mean you as an individual," Wendy said. "I mean men in general. As a group. I'm explaining why I feel the way I do, why I became anorexic. I thought you wanted to know."

"I guess I don't get the connection."

Wendy took a deep breath. "It's all to do with sex. That's what the doctor thought. You stop getting your period, you become asexual. And he said that's because I perceive men the way I just said. The trouble is, I'm also right! If it was just a matter of *perception*, it wouldn't matter. But I know that half the guys I meet either think I'm a freak or they just want to get some experience; they just want to stick their penis into someone so they can tell all their friends."

69

I would give the rest of my allowance till college if I could have this conversation on a video tape for Josie. I wouldn't even *go* to college. I'd become one of those hunched-over little guys who sells Super Hero comics in front of Bloomingdale's.

I had finished my cheesecake. "Girls are scary, too," I countered.

"In what way?"

"They can insult you, they can make you feel like a jerk after you've paid a lot of money taking them out. They can tear your ego to shreds just for the sheer fun of it."

Wendy looked at me thoughtfully. "Do you think that's what I've been doing?"

"Yes! And frankly, I'd just as soon you threw me in front of a subway train."

Wendy laughed. "I like your sense of humor, Charles."

"I'm glad I have some redeeming characteristics."

Wendy looked at me with a completely different expression. "I think you're a very honest, sensitive person. I appreciate your spending all that money. I would have paid for my ticket, but — "

"That's okay." I felt like a yo-yo that she was boinging up and down on a string.

I paid the check. Outside I hailed a cab. We rode back to Wendy's apartment in silence. I helped her out of the cab and took the elevator up to her apartment, 8A. "I'd ask you in," she whispered, "but it's sort of late."

I looked at my watch. It was one-fifteen. I guess

70

when you're being tortured, time passes quickly. I just stood there awkwardly.

"Would you like to kiss me good-night?"

"What's the penalty? Will you throw me in front of a subway train?"

Wendy smiled and leaned forward and we kissed each other.

God, I'm exhausted! I think this'll be my last date till I graduate medical school.

CHAPTER EIGHT

Monday I woke up with a sore throat and fever. Tuesday my fever was down a little, but Dad said I had to stay in bed another day. I dozed till around noon when Josie came into my room. "Had a rough date, huh?" she said.

"You better believe it," I said.

"Well, I had a really good time," she said, opening the venetian blinds.

"Stop it! Why're you doing that?" The light was blinding.

"Because you're going to get up and take a shower and change into clean pajamas. This room smells like a sewer."

"I'm at death's door. I have a fever."

Josie glanced at her watch. "It's twelve. Lunch is at twelve-thirty. Pajamas are proper attire if covered by a bathrobe."

My whole life has been warped by my being always surrounded by women of superhuman strength. No wonder I'm a neurotic mess. I should be getting a tray in bed. She's probably going to make me eat frog's legs with garlic. Actually, Josie had set up the kitchen table for me and Grandma, who was already gulping down her soup. She and Josie seemed to be getting along okay.

"Where's Dad?" I asked.

"He'll be home in half an hour. He's going to take Grandma for a walk."

I started in on Josie's chicken soup. "This is great. You were probably a Jewish mother in another life."

Josie snorted.

"Isn't the soup good, Granny?" I said, trying to get her to praise Josie.

"Delicious," my grandmother said. "They fired the other one." She munched on a cracker. "She stole my pearls. I had to hide everything! Samie fired her."

I looked at Josie who just shrugged. Evidently Grandma thought Josie was a different person. I wonder if it could be because of her wigs. But on the job Josie doesn't wear them much. Just when she's about to go out. She lives in a small apartment in the Bronx, and she goes home every night after dinner. I wanted to protest, but then I figured maybe if Grandma thought Josie was a new person, she'd treat her differently. "So, what's for dessert?" I said.

Josie was sitting at the marble table where she does her cooking, reading a cookbook. "There isn't any dessert. Have some fruit if you're still hungry."

I got up. "No Grand Marnier soufflé? No hazelnut torte à la Jacques Cousteau? Boy, the last cook we had would never have gotten away with just fruit, let me tell you." I found some navel oranges and peeled one. I offered a few sections to Grandma.

She took a section and began laboriously chewing and sucking on it. Her dentures sometimes get loose and she can't get a grip on food too well. "I don't

73

have anything left!" she exclaimed suddenly. "She took it all. She put it in a big black bag."

Josie gave a smothered laugh.

"What seems to be missing?" I said, trying to act calm and rational like my father.

"Everything! My clothes, my jewels, books, papers. She took it all. I told them. I said she comes in every day, pretending to clean. Nothing was clean. Everything was covered with dust. Why? Because she was so busy stealing. From your parents, from everyone."

I was beginning to feel uneasy at Josie's having to listen to all this. "Well, anyway, now there's this nice new lady to look after you," I said cheerfully.

My grandmother scowled at Josie and then, lowering her voice, said to me, "They're all the same. Don't tell me. She'll steal, too. They all steal. Clean your own house. That's the only way."

"Yeah, but Mom is busy, she works," I pointed out.

"She's never here," my grandmother said. "Always working. My poor Samie has nothing to eat. Nobody cooks for him. He's all alone. Why did he get married?"

"He got married because he fell in love with Mom," I said, beginning to get annoyed.

"Love!" My grandmother looked scornful. "Huh!"

"Anyhow, Dad gets plenty to eat," I went on. "You don't have to worry about him."

At that point I heard my father coming down the hall to the kitchen. "Who's worried about my appetite?" he said.

At the sight of my father, my grandmother's eyes lit up. She beamed. "Samie!"

"She thinks you're being neglected, that Mom and Josie don't take good enough care of you," I explained.

"It's true," my father said. "Look at me. All skin and bones, a shadow of my former self." He popped an orange section into his mouth. "How're you feeling, Charles?"

"Pretty weak, but okay. I took a shower."

"Good. Well, just rest up this afternoon and I'll take a look at you tonight. Come on, Granny. We're going out for a nice walk."

After they'd left, Josie said she would make both of us a cup of tea. "A big black bag," she snorted.

"What I don't get," I said, "is why she worships him. Do you worship your father that way?"

"My father's too drunk half the time to know up from down. Worship, my ass!" Josie stood over the tea kettle, waiting for it to boil.

"I get mad, hearing her talk about you that way."

"She's old. Leave her be." She grinned. "Tell me about your date instead. Did you have fun?"

"Fun?" I looked at her like she was crazy. "If you call being insulted and injured fun. Why do you think I'm sick? It's all psychological."

"A fever isn't psychological. Why were you insulting her? I thought I told you to treat her nice." Josie brought the two cups of tea over and sat down in my grandmother's place.

"I did! I treated her incredibly well. I bought great tickets for an excellent play. After it I took her to

Sardi's, this really elegant restaurant. You saw me, I wore my best suit. And suddenly she began lashing into me for *no* reason. She's just crazy."

"You must have said something," Josie said implacably, adding sugar to her tea.

"I didn't say *anything*. I was exceptionally polite, I groveled. I don't know, Josie, I think I've had it with women. They're too much trouble. I'm going to wait for college."

"College!" Josie gave me a disgusted look. "One date and you're quitting? Boy, where is your moral fiber?"

"Search me." I guess it got lost in the big black bag. The tea tasted good. I like being sick. If only I had rheumatic fever and could spend my life in bed with Josie cooking for me. I might become a great writer because I'd lie there all day having feverishly imaginative thoughts. I could teach Josie to take shorthand and she'd take it all down and type it up and we could split the royalties. Then at least she could get wigs made of real hair instead of that dynel plastic crap. "So, how'd it go with Willie?" I asked, just to put the shoe on the other foot.

Josie smiled. "Not bad. We went back to my place, had a few beers, played some cards — "

"You're not supposed to drink beer."

"*I* sipped. *He* drank. Don't you want me to have any fun out of life?"

"It's *your* liver. Okay, so then what? Did you, uh, do it?" I smirked.

Josie gave me a stern glance. "Did we do *what*?"

"You know. It." I made the sign for men and women fucking.

"Charles, now may I ask what business is that of yours? And where did you *get* such a perverse imagination? You don't come from a deprived home, you've been waited on hand and foot since the day you were born."

"Yeah, but I've been bossed around by women since the day I was born, too. It's sapped my will-power. And I'm a sixteen-year-old male. We're supposed to be obsessed with sex."

"You're supposed to be obsessed with *doing* it, not with hearing about other folks' sex lives."

"I'm a voyeur. What can I tell you? Sue me."

Josie stood up. "I know one thing you surely are: sick. In body as well as mind. Now, you heard your father. You get back in bed and rest! Your brother has his concert tomorrow and you better be well enough to go to that."

Oh shit. I forgot. Tomorrow Kaylo is playing Chopin's "Polonaise in A Major" at assembly. Josie's right. They'll skin me alive if I don't make it.

I guess my unconscious is more forgiving than my conscious. Maybe everyone's is. If you were rational all the time, you'd never get out of bed. Anyhow, I slept most of the afternoon and had feverish, erotic dreams about, of all people, Wendy Wolfe. Maybe I'm a masochist. Maybe I like being maltreated. When I got up, I felt rotten, much worse than before.

Josie peeked into the room. "There's a girl on the phone, Master Charles," she said.

77

Why is everyone so sarcastic in this house? Even when you're sick? Why did they free the slaves? Maybe we should get a robot instead. Master Charles! I went into the dining room, which was empty, and picked up the phone. "Hello?"

"Oh hi, Charles. It's Wendy. I was just worried about you because you haven't been in school for two days. I wondered if you were okay."

I'm a true softie. I should've just hung up, but I was touched that she'd noticed my absence. "Yeah, well, I'm pretty sick. I have a fever. It's some kind of virus."

"Do you think you'll make it tomorrow? Your brother's playing in assembly."

As though there was some danger I would forget! "I'm going to try. So how are you? I didn't infect you or anything, did I?" Then I realized that sounded kind of dirty, like I might have passed on some venereal disease.

"No, I feel fine. I'm just — Well, I'm sorry I got into all those heavy topics on our first date. It must have overwhelmed you. I bet you thought I was some fairly normal person."

"Never. I wouldn't go near a normal girl if you paid me."

Wendy giggled. "Anyhow, I just wanted to say I had a really good time."

I cleared my throat. "Maybe we can do it again sometime." What am I saying? Am I crazy?

"That'd be great. See you tomorrow." Next time you can try bringing your whips and chains and I'll jump through hoops.

Josie came into the dining room, carrying a big

78

heavy tray. She was setting the table for supper. "Was that the same one or some other one?"

"The same one. I guess she couldn't find anyone to torment in school."

Josie came closer. "You look worse."

"I am. I told you. I'm allergic to the female sex. One more date and I'll enter a monastery."

"Go take another shower. You look sweaty."

"Two showers in one day! I'll be so clean my antibodies won't have anything to hold on to."

I showered again. I always obey women when they order me around. I think when I was a baby, if I didn't do what they said, they would eat my animal crackers themselves or something despicably cruel like that.

CHAPTER NINE

That night I got into bed at nine. I felt exhausted, but not tired, if you know what I mean. Just wrung out. My mother came in to say good-night. "Do you think you can make it for Kaylo's concert?" she said. "I'll drive you when I go, at eleven."

"Sure, I'll try and make it." I tried to look as though not going would break my heart.

"You can just go for the concert and then we can go home. He'd be so disappointed if you didn't hear him."

Kaylo's rendering of Chopin will probably be the highlight of the season. He may get offered a round the world concert series. Maybe I can be his manager.

I tried to sleep and dozed off a little, but at two in the morning I was still up. The sheets felt hot and crumpled; so did my pajamas. Finally I got up. Passing my father's study I saw he was reading in his reclining chair, a glass of red wine and a burning cigarette in an ashtray on the side table. "I can't sleep," I said.

"Well, you slept all day. Lie down in here for a while. Maybe a change of scene will help."

I lay down on the green velvet couch in my father's study. It's short — I just about reach the end of it. I closed my eyes. Some classical music was on the radio. My father loves music so much. I wish I could be really good, good enough to make a profession of it. "Dad, I don't think I'm going to make it as a professional musician," I said. "I really don't think I have the stuff."

"So, you'll do something else."

He sounded so calm! "But how about all those lessons? Look at all that money you spent. What if you'd known all along I'd never make it, would you still have done that?"

"Sure. Your mother and I just wanted you to have the musical education our parents couldn't afford for us. What you choose to do with it is your own business. You can sing in a chorus, like your mother. You can sing in the shower."

"Maybe I can be Kaylo's manager."

My father reached over and patted my shoulder. "You'll be okay, Charles. I'm not worried about you."

He's not? Why isn't he? He should be! "But look at what a failure I am with girls! Look how fat and ugly I am!"

"How about that nice girl we met in the park? She seemed to like you."

"Yeah, but . . . she was just desperate. You said how skinny she was, remember?"

"She was a lovely girl," my father said. "Charles, relax. You'll meet someone, maybe not now. Maybe in college. If not in college, in medical school. You'll slim down. Adolescence is a time of trial and torment. People forget that. They only remember the good parts."

A time of trial and torment. Boy, that really hits it on the head. I like that. *The Adolescence of Charles A. Goldberg, A Time of Trial and Torment.* That sounds gripping. It could be a best-seller, if only it could end happily. I'll end it when I'm thirty-five and a world-famous, thin concert manager. "Ah, how far away those days seem, days with. . . ."

Just then Kaylo came into the room. He looked little and thin, much too little to be about to play Chopin's "Polonaise in A Major." "Daddy, Grandma's in my closet," he said in a quavering voice.

"What's she doing there?" Dad said.

"She's drawing on the walls with my magic markers. And she's saying funny things. I'm scared!" He burst into tears.

My father sighed. "Oh my God."

We both followed Kaylo into his room. He has a night light shaped like a duck, but his bedside light was also turned on. My father turned on the overhead light as well. He looked in the closet. My grandmother was in the back, carefully writing on the wall. "Granny, what are you doing?" my father asked very gently.

"Writing," came my grandmother's soft voice.

"What are you writing?"

"The story of my life."

My father got into the closet with my grandmother. "She's writing in Hebrew," he said heavily, either to himself or to us. To my grandmother he said, "Granny, I have a wonderful idea. Why don't you come into my study and I'll get you some paper and you can write it down so we can all read it."

82

"You want to read it?"

"Yes, we'd love to read it." He emerged from the closet with my grandmother. "Now first why don't we have a little snack?" This is a euphemism for giving her a few more Valiums. "Does anyone else here feel like a snack?"

"I do" whispered Kaylo. He still sounded subdued and shaky, unlike himself. He peeked into the closet at my grandmother's writing. I stood behind him. It was all crooked, going up and down one side of the wall in green magic marker writing. Since I don't know Hebrew, I don't know what it said.

In the kitchen my father gave Kaylo and my grandmother glasses of milk. Kaylo likes his with Strawberry Quik. I decided to be virtuous and just have an apple. "Let's wake Mommy up," Kaylo said. "Maybe she'd like a snack, too." He was sitting as far away from my grandmother as possible, not looking at her.

"No, I think we better let Mommy sleep," Dad said. He was eating a large chunk of chocolate halvah. He looked at my grandmother, whose eyes were drooping shut. "Okay, well, in the morning we'll get a special book for Granny's memoirs."

"I want to write *my* memoirs, too," Kaylo said. "Get *me* a special book, too."

"Okay. Two special books. How about you, Charles?"

"No, I think I'll wait till I'm illustrious."

"A wise decision."

My father got my grandmother and Kaylo back into bed. Then he came into my room. He sat on the edge of the bed. It was dark, but I could see his cigarette burning. "We're going to have to do something," he said.

"What do you mean?"

"She's getting impossible, scaring Kaylo. I don't know how much longer she can go on living here."

"You could put her in a home," I suggested.

"True." He was silent. I saw the tip of the cigarette glow more brightly. "I wondered if you'd do me a favor, Charles."

"Sure, Dad, what is it?"

"Well, I want to visit a few of these homes. I'd want one that would be close enough so I could visit every day, and the best one from that point of view is in the Bronx. Would you come with me?"

"Sure." I wondered why he'd want me along.

"Some of these places are hell holes. Sad, but true. I couldn't bear to put her in one of those."

I was too tired to reply.

For the next few moments my father sat in silence on the edge of the bed, finishing his cigarette. I must have fallen asleep while he sat there because when I came to again, it was morning and he was gone.

CHAPTER TEN

In the morning I felt marginally better. My fever was gone, but I felt as though little men with sandbags had been pummeling my body all night. I showered and got dressed. Mom peered in at ten-twenty. "You're sure you're up to it?"

"As long as I can come right back afterwards."

"Oh, of course. The minute it's over."

Dad was going to come, but he had an emergency consultation he couldn't get out of.

My mother's friend, Portia, the one she runs the catering service with, was coming, too. She's divorced and doesn't have kids. I don't mind Portia except for one thing: She has a doctorate in psychology and she's always going on about Freud this, Freud that. "How long have you been sick, Charles?" she asked in the car, turning to face the back where Mom had me quarantined.

I knew this was a no-win question. If I said, "Since my date with Wendy," she'd think it was because of an allergy to girls. If I said, "Since last night," she'd think I was jealous of Kaylo. "I'm basically fine," I said. "I just feel a little weak."

"He had a hundred and one," Mom said. "That's nothing to joke about. But I knew how badly Kaylo would feel if Charles didn't come. He worships him."

"That's sweet," Portia said, in a voice that implied she either didn't believe it or thought it was unbelievably neurotic.

Does Kaylo "worship" me? At times I feel he looks up to me, but no more than most little kids do to someone six years older than they are. It would be nice to think that to Kaylo, if to no one else in the family, I appear self-assured, competent, suave. I like to think of Kaylo lying in bed, thinking: One day I'll be as good as Charles at — But at what? What does he think I'm good at? Am I good at anything?

We arrived early, so my mother got us seats in the front row. Each assembly consists of three performances, usually kids of different ages, performing totally different kinds of things. Kaylo was the last on the program. First came a boy in the class below me who plays the trumpet. You may never have the opportunity to get out of a sick bed to hear a trumpet solo. If you ever do, I advise you to pass it up. The guy, Felix Fulmer, was probably as good at the trumpet as anyone can be, but face it, it's not an instrument you want to hear without accompaniment, even when you're in the best of health. Also, being in the first row, it felt like he was playing directly into my ear. Normally I try to sit as far back as possible. It's not from a musical point of view, it's just that the closer I am to the stage, the more I start noticing all the little nervous mannerisms of the person who's performing.

Sometimes I have to close my eyes, it bothers me so much. Felix's mannerism is he wiggles his ears. Once you notice that, you can't notice anything else. Since I was feeling pretty beat anyway, I closed my eyes.

I felt Portia give me a sharp nudge in the ribs. "You're snoring," she hissed.

God, how embarrassing. I wasn't even aware I was asleep. It just seemed like the trumpet was becoming soft and far away and almost pleasant.

Next came Lucius Sandler and Leah Broome doing a dance duet. I suppose seeing guys who're built like Lucius always makes me uncomfortable. There wasn't an ounce of fat on his body and, believe me, in those tights, you could see everything he had or didn't have. I'm sure I'd feel less jealous if he was gay, but he and Leah, who're in my class, have been going together forever. I'm surprised they haven't been married and divorced by now. Dancing can be sexy. Leah's on the skinny side, like Wendy, but the way she and Lucius wove together, in and out, started my mind on its usually round of X-rated filth. Maybe if I didn't know they were actually lovers my thoughts would've been more on the aesthetic side of the dancing.

I tried not to fall asleep, but even with my eyes half open I daydreamed. Lucius and Leah became Wendy and me, I was twirling and swaying her around in the air, she was gazing meaningfully into my eyes, people in the audience were thinking, "Wow, they must have a fantastic sex life." Maybe Josie's right. Am I a voyeur? Why do I care what people in the audience are thinking? Especially Portia and Mom. I glanced at them. They were watching attentively.

Then there was the big moment: Kaylo. Two guys pushed the giant black Steinway to the front of the stage. There was silence and finally Kaylo, in his best suit, walked briskly onto the stage and sat down on the piano stool, which had been twirled up so he could reach the keys. Actually, I don't think Kaylo gets that nervous, but I felt nervous for him. Here's this little kid, just four feet tall, with skinny little arms and legs. The piano looked enormous, like a dinosaur. But Kaylo just sat very still for a minute and then plunged right in. I had to admit I didn't enjoy a minute of it at first. I started feeling horribly queasy, almost like I might throw up. The piece has all kinds of fancy things where both hands do different things at the same time. I've heard Kaylo practicing, but it's different at home where you can go slowly or repeat if you make a mistake. I gripped the arms of my chair and felt sweat pouring down my neck.

When he was done, the place went wild. Maybe it was his age or maybe he's really that good, but they actually gave him a standing ovation. In a school like ours, where most of the kids are extremely talented, that's very rare. Kaylo just smiled modestly, bowed, ducked offstage, came back again, and then rushed off to join his class. One rule is that you rejoin your class, not your parents, after the performance. Mom was crying and she and Portia were hugging each other and acting like they hadn't seen each other since they got out of Auschwitz.

"How can he know so much?" Portia said. "So much about life? He's only ten!"

"I know," my mother said. "He has some kind of incredible intuition the minute his hands touch the keys. And yet in every other way he's just a normal, sweet little boy."

"You are so lucky, Megan," Portia said. "A child like that is born once a century, probably."

Whereas ones like me are born every three seconds, which may be why the world is in the shape it is.

Then Kaylo's piano teacher, Ms. Harazim, came rushing out, and she hugged Mom and started crying and the whole thing got going again. "Such feeling!" she said. "What a child! It's an honor to teach him. I am blessed to have him as a student."

I knew if I didn't make it to the men's room in one minute I would throw up all over the three of them. I ran out, murmuring, "Be back in a sec."

I made it in the nick of time. I stood there, dizzy. God, I felt lousy. Glancing in the mirror, I saw I looked even worse than I felt. I was slightly green or grayish green and my skin had a strange pasty look. But I felt a lot better after heaving my guts out — weak, but better. I ran into Kim as I was returning to the auditorium. "Charles! How come you're here?" he said. "I called your house and your grandmother said you were sick."

Granny isn't supposed to answer the phone. Naturally she forgot to tell me Kim called, but at least she got the information right. "I'm a lot better," I said. "I just came in for Kaylo. Mom insisted."

"He was fine," Kim said. "Too bad he rushed the adagio that way. But for his age. . . ."

Kim isn't the type to be bitchy. He just has perfect pitch and perfect honesty. "Did he get all the notes right?" I asked. "I wasn't listening that well."

Kim frowned. "A few errors here and there. He has trouble with his B flat, but he's fine, really good. I'm glad you could come. I'll call you tonight, okay?"

Kim wouldn't understand sibling rivalry if you sat down and explained it to him for an hour. He thinks families are people who root for you every inch of the way.

In the car on the way home I collapsed in the backseat. I could have been dying, but Mom and Portia were so busy babbling away about the concert they didn't even notice. "Is he going to that special camp you mentioned?" Portia asked.

"I think so," Mom said. "It's up to him. We don't want to pressure him. They have to practice four hours a day." She sighed. "This thing with Gustel has been so terrible for Kaylo. I just don't think Sam notices, or maybe he just denies it because she's his mother and he loves her so much."

"Terrible how?" Portia asked.

"Kaylo never had sleeping problems, *never*, totally unlike Charles, and now he has nightmares. His teacher told me his concentration is shot, he tells these strange stories about witches sitting on his bed at night. I'm afraid if we don't get her into a home soon, it'll really be a disaster."

"So, get her into one," Portia said. "What's the problem?"

"Sam thinks they're hellholes. He just won't face reality! Not everything has a perfect solution. His kids should come first."

Portia lowered her voice slightly. "How about Charles?" I think she figured I was asleep.

"It's hard to tell with him. Of course he's older, but he's always had problems." My mother sighed. "I don't know what we did wrong with Charles, but he seems so — "

"*I* think he seems much better," Portia said. "Remember how jealous he used to get when Kaylo got attention? Now he seems to almost take it in his stride."

Almost! I've been sick, you jerk! I've had a fever!

"If only he had his own thing!" Mom sighed. "Something *he* could excel in."

"But plenty of people don't excel in anything," Portia said, "and they go on to lead perfectly wonderful, normal lives."

"Somehow I can't see Charles — " my mother began.

"He's such a sweet boy," Portia said. "Frankly, I think he could be a real knockout, if he'd lose some weight."

A knockout? Why didn't I ever see this side of Portia before? Maybe she has a thing for younger men. I erased the rest of the conversation as too absurd to be worth contemplating. Anyone with their ears on straight could see I didn't have a ghost of a chance to lead a normal life, wonderful or horrible. But maybe I would be a knockout! When Portia left us at the door I hugged her so hard she almost fell off her feet. "See you!" I called gaily, waving good-bye.

In the elevator I said to Mom, "Portia's a really nice person. I can see why she's your best friend."

"She's not my best friend," Mom said. "She's a good friend. It's just a pity she has such problems with men. She always seems to pick the wrong ones."

"Wrong in what way?"

"Oh, either they're married or they don't treat her well, or they're too young."

"Too young for what?" I tried not to sound lascivious.

"Too young to take seriously," my mother said. "She's forty-two. She's too old to fool around with thirty-year-olds."

I gathered thirty-year-olds were considered "young." What did that make me? An infant in swaddling clothes? Still, she had said "a real knockout." That remark definitely saved the day.

At night, after dinner, Kaylo played his piece again for everyone so Dad and Grandma could hear it. I was feeling a lot better, especially since I'd slept all afternoon and could listen reclining on the couch. "I don't think you rushed the adagio as much as you did in assembly," I said.

"That's true," Kaylo said. "I had trouble with my B flat, too. Did you notice?"

"Only here and there," I said generously.

"Even Rubinstein made mistakes," Mom said.

"They said that was because he was so involved in the music."

Kaylo had insisted Mom bring the polacanthus into the living room to "listen" to the concert, too. "So, what're you going to be, Kay?" I asked. "A pianist or an expert on dinosaurs?"

"Both," he said firmly.

CHAPTER ELEVEN

By Thursday I was well enough to go to school. By Saturday I was well enough to tell Kim I'd take his little sister to the zoo with him. As I was leaving, my father stopped me. "Charles?"

"Yeah?"

"Remember what I said about our going together to look at some of those nursing homes for Gustel?"

"Uh huh. When do you want to go?"

"Well, I'm going to look at some today, but I thought maybe next Saturday we might visit the one in the Bronx. The others are so terribly far away."

"Will she, uh, come with us?"

Dad looked horrified. "No, of course not. She'd be terrified. You must never mention it, never. Do you understand?"

I was taken aback. "Okay. Is Mom coming?"

My father looked away. "No, I . . . I'd rather do it alone. It's my mother and — But if you'd rather not come, I'd understand."

"Why do you want *me* to come?" That was the part I didn't get.

He looked right at me. "Moral support."

On the way to Kim's I thought about that and

wondered what my father meant. Why would I lend moral support? What do I know about nursing homes or anything else? And why would my father need moral support? Usually I think of him as pretty self-sufficient, a loner almost. I figured whatever moral support he needed, he got from my mother. I can tell he doesn't want to do this and I don't blame him. My grandmother won't know where she is. She gets scared even in our house if my father isn't around. There she'd just be with total strangers. Sometimes I'll remember my grandmother the way she used to be, so perky and lively and interested in things.

Till she was seventy-five, even, my grandmother never fit into the stereotype of a little old lady. She used to play tennis all the time. She'd just go to the public courts and pick up a game with people half her age. She always had this fearless or maybe iconoclastic streak. Like, no matter how late it was when she went home from our apartment, she'd take a bus, never a cab. When there was a bus and subway strike in New York City, she would pick up strangers on the street and drive them home, even into Harlem. Mom and Dad used to worry about her, but she said she was old enough to know what she was doing.

But it's getting harder and harder for me to connect that person with the one who lives with us. In a way it's as though my real grandmother had died and this other person is standing in for her, but not doing a very convincing job, forgetting her lines, wearing the wrong costumes. What's it like for her?

Does she remember the way she used to be? Maybe it's only weird for the people who are watching and remembering.

Kim's parents run a fruit and vegetable market on Madison and Seventy-eighth. They used to have one further uptown, but it did very well and they got some kind of write-up in *New York* magazine and *The New York Times,* so about a year ago they moved. Kim says it's tense because the rent is prohibitively high. It's almost more like a museum than a fruit and vegetable market. Everything is washed and polished and set out so you more want to admire the produce as works of art than eat them. Above each fruit or vegetable Kim's mother, Mrs. Huong, writes in very delicate beautiful script, "Green pepper," and then the Latin word and then the price. Mr. Huong stands in front, behind the cash register. He always wears a business suit. It makes him look like a Wall Street broker.

Kim's sister, Soo Li, is eight. She's slim and delicate-looking, like their mother, and doesn't talk much. He also has an older sister at MIT who's getting a degree in electrical engineering. Kim and Soo Li were waiting outside the store when I arrived. Kim's grandfather was with them. He's small and even more delicate-looking, but, except for the fact that he's almost blind and carries a cane, you'd never guess he was eighty-seven. Five years older than my grandmother! "Grandfather would like to come with us," Kim said. "Okay?"

"Terrific."

That meant we had to walk slowly, but I didn't

mind. Grandfather, as they call him, walked ahead with Soo Li, and Kim and I took up the rear. "How's your grandmother doing?" Kim asked. He hasn't been over to our apartment since that night she fell.

"Fair," I said. "My father is thinking of putting her in a home. He thinks it's the only solution."

I looked ahead at Kim's grandfather. It seems so unfair that some people age and remain the same people. They just get weaker or smaller or whatever, but their personalities are pretty much the same. I guess, when you come down to it, what bothers me the most about my grandmother is she doesn't seem to have the same personality. It isn't so much that her intellectual capacities are dwindling or that she forgets things. "She's writing her memoirs," I said. I meant it as a kind of joke, though actually my father did go out and buy her a black notebook to write in so she wouldn't write on the walls anymore.

"Grandfather should do that," Kim said. "He remembers so much about a time that seems a million years ago." To his grandfather he repeated, in a louder voice, "Charles was saying I should buy you a book . . . to write down your past."

Kim's grandfather smiled. He tapped his head. "But I have it all up here."

"For other people," Kim said.

"No one cares," his grandfather said sadly. "They want to forget."

"No, you should do it," Kim said. But when his grandfather had gone ahead, he said more quietly, "Maybe he's right. My parents say they want to forget the past, too. They think otherwise you can spend your whole life clinging to it. They say: Look ahead."

"Mr. Morantz says, if you forget the past you're condemned to repeat it." That's our history teacher.

"Doesn't he mean countries, not individuals?"

"Maybe it applies to both." Though maybe if you have a good memory like Kim's grandfather, it's like having a million movies stored in your head. Whatever mood you're in, you take one out and play it. He's right. Why write it down? That might spoil it, fix it a certain way. Whereas if it's just in your mind, you can always change it around.

We went to the zoo, but Soo Li said she wanted to stay outside. I was glad. If I was an animal in a zoo — I know I only look like one most of the time — I'd much rather be one of the ones who're out-of-doors, like the seals or the polar bears. The ones that depress me the most are the monkeys and apes in the monkey house. The stench in there is something fierce. Maybe they don't notice or maybe to them it's a good, even appealing smell. I'm not sure how I feel about zoos in general. I know some are better than others and how would kids and people in general get a chance to see real wild animals otherwise? But there's nothing worse than seeing some large, graceful animal like a tiger just lying there with its head on its paws. He's safe, it's true, no predators, but he's got to be thinking at some level that this isn't the life he was born to lead.

But then who isn't thinking that most of the time?

Soo Li laughed delightedly when the zoo keeper tossed the fish to the seals. We'd arrived just in time for their lunch. They never missed. She was holding Kim's grandfather's hand. "Soo Li can swim just like this," he said. "Like a fish."

She looked up at him and smiled. "I am a fish."

"And I am a seal. I will swallow you up."

"And I'll jump out again." She giggled.

They moved closer to get a better view while Kim and I stood in the background. I put my sunglasses on because the sun was pretty bright. "It's funny," Kim said. "Sometimes I think they're like a couple, Soo Li and Grandfather. They're together all the time. She brings him his tea in the morning. At night she sits in his room doing her homework."

"Families break up into groups like that," I said, thinking of ours.

"It's like that with me and my mother," Kim said, "and my father and my older sister. She says he's the only one she can talk to about her work. I feel my mother is the only one who listens to me when I talk. My father pretends to listen, but he doesn't really listen. He only cares if what I do will lead to my making a good living."

"Sounds familiar." We bought some Cracker Jacks and Cokes from a stand. I thought of our family. Oddly, when I think of it in the terms Kim was talking about, I think our family breaks down to Kaylo and my mother, my father and my grandmother, and me and Josie. What I mean by that is just if there's one person to whom I feel I can tell anything, absolutely anything, it's probably Josie, even though she's as tough on me as a Marine sergeant. Of course, it breaks down in other ways, too. Like, sometimes Kaylo and I are buddies and sometimes my parents are pretty close-knit and don't want anyone else around. But that's the way it's supposed to be. I think Kim meant the patterns most people wouldn't notice beneath the surface.

"The seals are stuffed," Kim's grandfather said.

"How do you know?" Soo Li asked. "Maybe they didn't get enough. Maybe they're still hungry."

"I think someone else is hungry," Kim's grandfather said.

"Not for raw fish," Soo Li said, and wrinkled her nose.

We ended up at the zoo cafeteria where we could sit outside under an umbrella. "This is a beautiful park," Kim's grandfather said. "It reminds me of Korea."

Kim stood up. He had his Minolta around his neck. He brings it everywhere. He began moving in close for a picture of the three of us. "Not me," Kim's grandfather said. "I'm too old."

"No, you're not," Kim said. "Soo Li, move a little closer."

"Then I'll be sitting in his lap!"

"Sit in his lap, then."

Kim was clicking away while he talked. Usually his photos come out extremely well because he keeps shooting, even while he's talking. I figured at least my sunglasses would conceal part of my face. I was wearing a gaudy shirt with huge plants on it that Mom got me in Hawaii.

Kim's grandfather pointed at me. "Charles is the most colorful. Take some of Charles."

Kim aimed at me. "If you were smoking a cigarillo, you'd look like a plantation owner."

I stood up. "Do you want me to take some of the three of you?"

"Sure." Kim handed me the camera. It's like the one Dad gave me a couple of years ago, but I hardly ever use mine. I think one problem is I forget I have it — it's in the back of the closet — and another is I spend so much time focusing and waiting for the perfect shot, that people get disgusted.

"How is your brother?" Kim's grandfather asked. "I hear he gave a fine concert the other day."

"He's a musical prodigy," I said dismissively.

"Like Kim," said Soo Li.

"I don't like the word *prodigy*," Kim said. "Kaylo's talented, but I thought you said he wants to study dinosaurs."

"He's only ten," I said, sipping my iced tea. "Too young to know what he really wants."

"I'm eight," Soo Li said. "And I know what I want to be . . . a harpist."

I looked over at her. She really is lovely, with silky black hair and soft, melting black eyes. Maybe I should get her together with Kaylo. Maybe that's what he needs, a sweet, quiet girl friend. Actually, maybe that's what I need. Will she wait for me? She's eight, I'm sixteen. Ten years from now I'll be a suave, accomplished twenty-six. I could arrange her first concert tour. Actually, there's also Kim's older sister, Sung Wu, but first, I think she considers me a little punk, and second, she's been horribly Americanized. She has as many opinions as Wendy.

Soo Li and Kim's grandfather went to see the

polar bears. Kim and I said we'd meet them back at the cafeteria. We just sat there comfortably, not talking much. I wonder if that's possible with a girl — to just sit, not feeling you have to entertain, not feeling you're being judged or held up to some hideous, unmeetable standard. If Kim were a girl, would I like him? Probably not; it wouldn't be this comfortable. He'd strike me as weird and incomprehensible. I'd wonder what he was thinking right now, gazing off into the distance. "I went out with Wendy Wolfe," I said, figuring I might as well tell him.

"I saw you talking to her in school," Kim said. "How was it?"

"She's kind of strange."

"And you are not?" Kim smiled.

"I need someone passive, bovine, silent."

"But you love to talk!"

"Someone who'll listen, who won't give me her damn opinions all the time. Why do girls have so many opinions? Maybe I should look for a deaf mute."

Kim looked horrified. "I want someone I can talk to," he said, "more than anything. Someone who'll be supportive, but who tells me the truth, too. Like, when my father wanted to buy this new store, he talked it over with my mother for months. She didn't just nod and smile. She told him what she really thought. If she had thought he shouldn't do it, he wouldn't have."

"Right, I guess it would be good to get advice. But I don't know. I think I'll be a bachelor. It's less trouble."

Kim looked surprised. "You don't want children?"

"Naw, not especially. Why? Just to carry on my twisted, perverse family genes?"

"Sometimes I think you're vain about being perverse," Kim said. "Deep down you're afraid you're normal, that some girl will find out if you get too close to her."

"You've got to be kidding." What is this? The wisdom of the Orient? What does he know? He's never been out with anyone!

Kim was smiling at me. "Wendy is pretty."

"She's fair. Up close she's more peculiar-looking. Her bottom teeth are crooked. And she has weedy arms. She used to be anorexic."

Kim stood up. "I would hate any girl to hold me to such a high physical standard," he said dryly.

We went to join Soo Li and Kim's grandfather.

CHAPTER TWELVE

The next morning, just as I was about to leave for school, Kim called and said his grandfather had died. He said he just came home from the zoo, had an early dinner, went to sleep, and never woke up. God, I can't believe that! Less than twelve hours ago he was sitting right there, joking and talking and walking around. He looked fine!

"It was a good way to go," Kim said quietly. "He was getting very frail. Soo Li is extremely upset, of course."

I went into the kitchen where Kaylo and my mother were having breakfast. She takes us both to school Mondays. "Kim's grandfather just died," I said, still feeling stunned.

"Right this second?" Kaylo said, munching on his cereal.

"Weren't you at the zoo with him yesterday?" Mom said. She only has black coffee in the morning. She was sipping it, already dressed in a polka-dot dress.

"Yeah, that's what's so weird. He *seemed* fine. Now he's just gone."

"But he was eighty-seven."

"Still." I couldn't seem to explain what I meant. I wasn't even sure what I meant. Would I have acted differently yesterday if I'd known that yesterday was his last day on earth? It wasn't like I did anything wrong, but I hadn't really thought about him much. In fact I was glad when he and Soo Li went off to see the polar bears so I could talk to Kim about Wendy. I didn't really want to hear him go on about the old days in Korea.

Just then my grandmother came wandering into the kitchen in her pajama top. She wasn't wearing anything on her bottom half. She started sitting down in a chair, but my mother grabbed her and said, "Gustel, please get dressed before you come in for breakfast. Do you want me to show you where your clothes are?"

"My clothes?" My grandmother looked surprised, as though, in her opinion, she was properly clad.

"Yes, please come on. We're in a hurry. I have to take the boys to school." My mother propelled my grandmother out of the room.

The minute they left Kaylo looked horrified. "Grandma was naked!"

"Only half naked."

He bent over close to me. "I once saw Mom like that when I was little. She took me in the ladies' room, and told me not to look, but the door didn't lock, and I peeked."

"Was it a big thrill?"

"Yeah."

I've seen my parents naked and it decidedly was not a thrill. They're both in horrible shape. The thought of them engaging in any act requiring close physical proximity is repugnant to me. I hope they do it in the dark. I'm certainly going to. Or maybe I'll stay under the covers but have the girl, Wendy, say — No, wait, I have a better idea. I'll make her swear to keep her eyes closed, only I'll keep *mine* open. But why would she agree to that? I'd tell her I'm modest. Oh come on, with Wendy's views on men, I won't get within ten feet of her. That kiss better last me till I turn twenty.

"Is Grandma crazy?" Kaylo asked suddenly.

"No, she's just. . . . She forgets things. It's just what happens to some people when they get old."

"Will it happen to Mom and Dad?"

"Not necessarily. Anyway, not for a long time and maybe never." I tried to sound more reassuring than I actually felt.

He was still looking scared. "Will it happen to us?"

"Kay, listen, say your best friend is hit on the head by a rock, does that mean you're going to be hit on the head? This is just Grandma, it's a thing that happened to her, the way some old people get rheumatism or whatever."

Kaylo was hunched over, staring at his plate. "I wish she'd gotten some other thing."

"So does everyone."

I watched him. He was staring down at his plate, like he was in another world. Then, a minute later, he looked up and in a totally different voice said, "I want to have a girl friend."

"Well, you're too young," I snapped. "I don't even have one and I'm sixteen."

"How come?"

"How come what?"

"You don't have one."

"There are more interesting things to do than be with girls." Yeah? Like what?

"I can't think of anything except piano, dinosaurs, and swimming," Kaylo said. The brutal honesty of the young.

My mother came rushing back into the kitchen. "She's getting dressed," she said. "But we have to go. Kaylo, you only ate half your cereal!"

"I was talking to Charles," he said importantly.

"About what?"

"Girls."

In the car my mother turned to both of us, but especially Kaylo. "Darling, you mustn't let the way Grandma is upset you. She can't help it. She just doesn't remember things."

"That's okay," Kaylo said. "It's just the way some old people get. Only I thought she was supposed to wear diapers." That's a kind of pad my grandmother wears under her pants. They're called dignity pads.

"She is, but she forgets."

"I used to wear diapers," Kaylo informed us. "And I used to wet my bed."

I remember. His room stank. It was awful.

"But now you're a big boy," my mother said. "But with Grandma it's the opposite. There are things she used to know how to do and now she's forgetting. It's like going backwards."

Kim didn't come to school that day. I guess he was home helping his mother. All I could think about all day, it seemed, was his grandfather and my grandmother, how different they were, wondering what I'd be like at that age, what my parents would be like. When Wendy sat down next to me in the cafeteria, I just looked at her glumly. "Kim's grandfather died," I told her.

Obviously that didn't mean much to her because she never knew him, so I told her about what he was like and how we'd gone to the zoo. She listened in a kind of preoccupied way, as though she was thinking about something else. "So, do you feel like coming over to my house after school?" she said when I was done, as though that had some connection to what I'd been saying.

"What for?"

Wendy turned red. "Just to . . . we could do our homework. You didn't seem to understand what Mrs. Katz was saying about Virginia Woolf that well. I could help you."

"Sure, well, why not?" I wondered if "do our homework" was a euphemism for making out. I wish I was more worldly. I forgot about Kim's grandfather. This could be my big moment, or even a small moment.

Wendy's apartment wasn't half as big as ours, but it was neater and more elegant-looking. Her room was smaller than mine, too, and only fairly messy. She had what looked like an exceptionally narrow bed. I guess she thought I was looking at the stuffed snake she had at one end of the bed because she said, "That's Sylvester. I know I'm too old for stuffed animals, but. . . ."

Pretty phallic, a stuffed snake. Now we know where her real thoughts lie. Still, I decided to play

108

it extraordinarily cool because of all that she said last time. I don't want to be an easy lay, after all. She'll have to beg and plead, even for a kiss.

But, surprisingly, Wendy just leaned over and kissed me. No lead up. No remark. I was startled. "Um . . . how come you invited me over?" I blurted out.

"What do you mean?"

"I mean, was it because you want to make out or what?"

Wendy looked acutely embarrassed. "I just wanted to show you I'm not . . . that I think there are exceptions." Her voice had dropped very low.

"To what?"

"To what I said about boys. That some of them are different."

I didn't know what to say. I'm not sure I am different.

"I get the feeling you're not used to being with girls that much," Wendy said. "But I think I'm different, too."

Probably it was my hormones or being alone in her small room, sitting on her narrow bed while she stroked Sylvester, but I began feeling rampantly and absurdly horny. I'm *not* different! I'm the same! Probably worse. But I decided to make a bold move. I put my arms around Wendy and kissed her gently on the lips. "We can do the homework later."

I'm not good at porno stuff, so all I can say is what happened was good. But to be scrupulously honest, it didn't go much beyond kissing and some groping around, mainly above the waist. The size of her breasts became less important than the fact of their existence. We stopped when we heard the door slam and her mother call, "Wendy, are you home?"

Wendy jumped up. "Yes, I'm here . . . with Charles. We're doing homework." Quickly we got our books out and opened them so that when her mother entered the room a few minutes later, it looked like a reasonable facsimile of two students working.

"Why, hello, Charles. How nice of you to help Wendy with her homework."

I just smiled.

"I'll leave you to your labors." She snapped on the overhead light. "Perhaps this might help a little."

After she'd left Wendy scowled. "That's *so* sexist! *You* helping *me*, not me helping you! And here you're practically flunking and I'm an A student!"

"I'm not practically flunking." There was just one exam where I was too tired to concentrate, but since then my grades have improved dramatically.

"But do you see what I mean?" Wendy pursued. "Why did she assume, without any evidence, that it was *you* helping *me*?"

"Maybe she's just sensitive to the male ego," I suggested. I picked up Sylvester. As stuffed snakes go, he's kind of cute. Maybe I should get one for Kaylo.

"How about the female ego?" Wendy fumed. "*We* don't have them? It's removed at birth?"

Uh oh. Here we go again. I thought of half an hour before, Wendy's soft lips, her breasts, her quiet breathing and murmuring. That was the real Wendy, this was her impersonator. "Do you think she knew what we were really doing?" I asked anxiously.

"You mean the way she turned on the light?" Wendy glanced at the door. "Probably. But she likes you, for some reason. She's probably relieved I'm in here with a guy instead of. . . ."

"With a girl?"

"No! Not with a girl! Charles, why do you make dumb remarks like that? Do you think I'm gay?"

I was getting irritated. "Well, why do you? 'She likes you, for some reason.' Maybe she likes me because she sees I'm an intelligent, sensitive, brilliant guy who has just a few problems, which a modicum of female attention and encouragement might cure."

Wendy giggled. She kissed the tip of my nose. "You're funny," she said affectionately.

Why do girls think I'm funny when I'm being totally serious?

Wendy was still gazing at me. "Do you want me to explain *To the Lighthouse*, or do you want to go home?"

"Are those my only two choices?" I moved closer to her and put my arm around her.

Wendy looked around nervously. "Well, now that Mom's home. . . . Anyway, I'm worried that if you don't understand it, you'll flunk the exam tomorrow."

I looked horrified. "There's an exam tomorrow?"

"Yes! Didn't you hear her at the end of the period? Two essay questions out of three."

God, I'm getting worse than my grandmother.

I didn't hear *anything* about an exam. "Okay, well, just explain it very simply. My brain is all out of condition." What I really meant was that making out with Wendy had done something to the supposed rational part of my brain, given it a shot of Novocaine as it were. If I ever lose my virginity, I'll be like someone with a prefrontal lobotomy. They may have to lock me up.

"It's mainly two images of women," Wendy explained. "Mrs. Ramsey is the ideal mother, the way Virginia Woolf thought of her own mother who died when she was young. She takes great care of her own kids, but she's being eaten alive by having nothing but her family and her domineering idiot husband."

"God, that really sounds grim."

"Didn't you read the book?" Wendy looked at me intently.

"Kind of."

"Well, look at it again tonight because I'm just giving you the general picture, not the fine points. Then there's Lily Briscoe. She's the artist who has nothing but her art. She never marries, but she has an inner self because she hasn't squandered it on her family."

It was beginning to sound like some kind of feminist tract. "I thought it was about getting to the lighthouse." I tried to look thoughtful and intellectual.

"It is, but the lighthouse is a symbol. Of how things are never really the same once they really happen, of how things diminish as you get older, how your parents seem less terrific, how nothing really is what you hope it'll be."

Jesus, this is getting really depressing. Why do they give this stuff to impressionable kids like us? "Do you think that's true?"

"Probably partly."

"Do you think it'll be true of sex, even?"

Wendy smiled. "Is that all you ever think about, Charles?"

I looked sheepish. "No, actually I hardly ever think about it, except when I'm awake. Well, I guess I don't have to worry. No one's ever going to want to do it with me anyway — have sex, that is, not go to the lighthouse."

Wendy hugged me. "Charles, I am naive about guys, but that's a line no one over the age of eight would fall for."

"It wasn't a line!" I cried, my voice rising and cracking. "It's the truth!"

"If you're so interested in sex, why're you going out with *me*?" Wendy demanded. "Why not Teresa Brewer or Nancy O'Brien?"

"I just have this strange attraction to skinny girls who like to sleep with stuffed snakes. Probably Freud would understand it."

Wendy stood up. "We have dinner in half an hour. I have to wash my hair. Call me if there's anything else you don't understand, okay?"

I guess Wendy's a good teacher. I got an A-minus on the exam. "Fine analysis, Charles," Mrs. Katz wrote. "I'm glad to see you're paying attention in class. Welcome back!"

CHAPTER THIRTEEN

The next Saturday was the one Dad and I were going to the nursing home in the Bronx. Josie was going to stay home and look after Grandma. Kaylo had a date at a friend's house.

"How's it going with Willie?" I asked Josie just before we set out. I was grabbing a quick snack to give me fortitude.

"He's not my type. You were right. He's too old. I need someone with a little more pep. How about you and that girl on the planning board?"

I smirked. "We're still planning . . . family planning."

Josie looked shocked. "Charles, you don't mean that you're — "

"Relax. We're just doing a little experimental foreplay. Nothing to get excited about. The kind of thing you were probably doing at Kaylo's age."

"And how do you know about when I was doing anything?" She picked up her meat chopper and brandished it menacingly.

"Well, you grew up on a farm, didn't you? I thought farm kids were precocious."

"I can tell you one thing. If any of us had ever talked the way you do, we wouldn't have lived to do much of anything."

I could tell she was making meat loaf for dinner, not my favorite. "That's my point. With me it's all verbal. Once I really start doing anything, I'll shut up about it."

Josie began mushing the meat and raw egg together. "You're never going to shut up unless they operate on your vocal cords, boy."

Dad came in and repeated to Josie all the instructions about Granny, what she should do if this happened or that happened. Josie sat there impassively, listening. I knew she was thinking she'd heard it all a dozen times, but maybe my father has some kind of male authority that I don't. She never talks back to him. "When should I expect you back?" she asked when he was done.

"Three, four. . . . If she gets anxious, the — "

"Valium are in the top drawer in the bedroom," Josie finished for him.

My father looked harassed and anxious in one of his usual crumpled gray suits. You can put the best tailored suit in the world on him and in ten minutes it looks like someone had rolled over it with a tanker. I was wearing my Hawaiian shirt and chinos. Dad looked at me with concern. "Is that what you're going to wear?"

"Yeah, any objections?"

He sighed. "Well, maybe it'll cheer the old folks up, who knows."

We went to the garage where my parents keep their Chevy. I got in next to Dad and put on my sunglasses. It wasn't too sunny, but I think they make me look sophisticated. I wish I knew how to drive. Driving isn't a big deal in Manhattan the way it is in most parts of America. It's not like a status symbol, do you have this car or that. Still, I should learn. My connection to male sexual rites is tenuous enough as it is. I have to start learning the art of bonding with mechanical objects.

"This may be an ordeal," my father said as we turned onto the West Side Highway.

"Why?"

"I'm just so afraid. . . ." He stopped. "Well, it's foolish to start in on fears before we get there. It may be a wonderful place. Maybe we'll check in ourselves."

He didn't talk much for most of the drive. I could tell he was thinking about what lay ahead. I mainly thought about Wendy. It's amazing how, even when she's giving me some tedious lecture on *To the Lighthouse*, I sit there absolutely mesmerized, like it was the most fascinating, wonderful thing in the world. Partly it's her eyes. She's saying all these awful things about men and how terrible they are while her eyes are beaming totally different signals like: Take my clothes off, kiss me, make love to me. Or is that just my overworked adolescent imagination?

The nursing home was a regular brick building, like an apartment house — several buildings, in fact. First we went in and Dad spoke to some woman who ran the place named Ms. Delisio, who said what a great place it was, and how there was a waiting list and how you could visit as often as you wanted. "Since you're a doctor, you'll appreciate how sanitary we keep everything," she said. "You know how old people are. We insist they wash once a day and we wash everything, even their blankets, once a week."

My father was staring at her with an unreadable expression. "Could we see the facilities?" he asked.

"I'd like a little information about your mother's physical and mental condition, Dr. Goldberg," Ms. Delisio said. "I believe you said on the phone that she has periods of being severely disoriented. Is it what you would diagnose as Alzheimer's?"

"Yes," my father said.

"Well, in that case, Mrs. Goldberg would be on the fourth floor, which is where we put our patients with Alzheimer's. They can participate in all the activities of the Center, if they wish. But they must be accompanied at all times."

My father nodded.

"Perhaps after your visit, you'd like to return here and ask some more questions. This is always a hard decision to make, but we have a file of letters from grateful children who testify to the excellence of our facilities. Our whole aim is to make our patients as happy as is possible under the circumstances."

When she said "children" I thought of kids Kaylo's age, but then I realized she meant people my father's age.

For some reason at that point she looked at me. I was still wearing my sunglasses. I took them off. "Will you come with me?" she said crisply.

The first couple of floors were just like the Senior Citizen's Center my grandparents used to visit in Florida. There were old people who looked the way my grandparents used to look, kind of peppy and cheerful, playing cards or Ping-Pong, painting. "We have quite a Ping-Pong tournament going," Ms. Delisio said. "Mr. Widman has won three years running, but I think this year Mrs. Rodriguez is giving him a run for his money."

Mrs. Rodriguez came up to me, racket in hand. "Want to play, sonny?"

"Maybe later." She'd probably slaughter me. Anyway, I hate playing Ping-Pong with women who have moustaches.

Finally we got to the fourth floor. It seemed a lot quieter than the other floors. We looked in one room and a bunch of ladies were lined up, some in wheelchairs, just staring straight ahead. It was like a bunch of seagulls on a fence. When we walked in, some looked at us and others kept staring straight ahead. "This is the main lounge," Ms. Delisio said. "The TV is in the corner and the list of each day's events is posted in the corner. If you'd like to look around, I'll just nip in and have a talk with our head nurse."

My father and I wandered around the room. No one was playing cards, they were just sitting. As we passed one table, a little old lady jumped up and grabbed my father's arm. "Doctor, doctor, where is he?" she cried. "Where did he go?"

I wondered how she knew my father was a doctor. "Where did who go?" he asked in that gentle voice he uses with my grandmother.

"My son. . . . He said he'd come. He isn't here! I don't know where I am." She looked terrified.

"Maybe he's coming later in the afternoon," my father said, sitting down opposite her.

"But I've been waiting and waiting. Where am I? Tell me where I am! Did they take me back to Germany? They don't seem to understand the language." She began saying something in Yiddish.

My father answered her in Yiddish.

"You know him?" the old lady cried, gripping my father's arm. "You know my son? You'll tell him?"

Just then Ms. Delisio came marching into the room. "What seems to be the matter, Mrs. Braunstein?" she asked sternly.

"My son, my son. . . ." The old lady looked scared again.

"Now, you know your son is no longer alive," Ms. Delisio said. "He's been dead for a year. Remember? You went to his funeral."

"My son died?" The old woman looked at me and my father for corroboration, as though disbelieving, as though it were the first time she'd heard it. "But he was a young man!"

"He was in a car accident," Ms. Delisio said implacably.

"But he didn't drive!"

"Someone else was driving."

The old lady started to shake. "He was young!" She grabbed my father's hand. "I want to see him. Just one more time."

"Nurse Hammonds! Nurse Hammonds!" called Ms. Delisio.

A moment later a small Puerto Rican woman in a white uniform darted into the room. "Please take Mrs. Braunstein into her room," she said. "It's time for her nap."

Nurse Hammonds dragged Mrs. Braunstein into her room. Although my father hadn't said anything, Ms. Delisio said defensively, "We can't watch all of them all the time. We just don't have the staff. The ones who are violent are watched more carefully. But we make sure they're clean and take their medicine. And you can visit as often as you like."

We walked around the rest of the floor, but it was pretty much the same: rows of old ladies, sitting, staring off into space. My father was silent. He looked gray. He took his pack of cigarettes out of his pocket. His hands were trembling. Ms. Delisio touched his hand. "I'm sorry, Dr. Goldberg. We don't allow smoking. Do you have any further questions?"

"We'll be in touch," my father said. He walked briskly out of the building and drew out the pack of cigarettes the second he was outside. "Let's go get something to eat."

We didn't know the neighborhood and ended up at a local bar where we both ordered draft beer and corned beef sandwiches, with pickles on the side.

"What did you think?" he asked me.

"Well, I guess it's as good as it can be," I said. "I mean, I wouldn't want to marry Ms. Delisio, but she probably wouldn't want to marry me, either." I thought I might joke my father into a less grim mood, but he just stared blanky ahead.

"It's nightmarish," he said.

"The place or getting that way?"

"Both. If I ever get that way, promise to shoot me, okay?"

"Then I'd go to jail."

"Then I'll shoot myself."

Boy, this was a depressing conversation! "Couldn't you just take an overdose?" I said, trying to sound lighthearted. "Guns are kind of messy."

"Okay, I'll take an overdose." For some reason that decision seemed to cheer Dad up. "This is wonderful beer," he said. "Can you taste the difference?"

"Between what and what?"

"Between draft and bottled. Draft has that wonderful freshness." He sighed. "I feel better." He looked right at me. "Thanks for coming with me, Charles. You don't know how much that meant to me."

"Sure, well, any time."

"Megan didn't get along with her mother. She can't understand what this is like for me. My mother — I wouldn't be here if it weren't for my mother. You wouldn't be here. She got my father over from Russia with no money. She got a job with no education and no training. She used to go to the homes of these wealthy society ladies and she'd rub their foreheads, their shoulders, and, bingo, all their migraines and tensions and neuroses would fly out the window. Sort of like what today we'd call holistic medicine."

I bit into a pickle. Usually I feel pretty skeptical of that kind of thing. "Do you think it really worked, or they just thought it did?"

"Both, like anything. Cheaper than a shrink, and I think they admired her. Here they were, pampered from the day they were born, going to pieces if a nail broke, and there she was, getting a family over from Europe, supporting the family. She used to bring me along. I'd 'tutor' the sons of the family who were flunking out of Andover or Loomis or wherever. Big fat hunks who could barely read comic books. I'd fool around with them and try to stuff in the odd fact. We'd set outrageous fees and the mothers always paid. Money was like water to them. It would never give out. That's how Granny sent us all to college, me to medical school."

"How about Grandpa?" I said. Dad was right, the beer was sensational or maybe it was just the whole atmosphere, the two of us, having a man-to-man talk in the dark bar, escaping from that prison of scared little old ladies.

"He was a nonentity." Dad half smiled. "No, that's too harsh, perhaps. But he didn't have her drive, her vision. If she hadn't been there, we'd never have gotten anywhere. That's why this is so hard for me. I hate to see what's become of her. She was someone who would stay up, after an eleven-hour workday, till four reading. She'd buy books before she'd buy food. She did everything. She would have given her life for any of us, but more than that, she just gave us the feeling that we could make it, no matter what the odds."

Maybe that's something that skips generations. I certainly don't think I can make it; I guess I'm more like those idiot boys my father used to tutor. Maybe after that first generation all the drive oozes away and you're left with sons like me. "So, will you put her in that home?"

"I don't know. What do you think I should do?"

This was the first time in my life my father had

ever asked me a question as though he cared about my answer. Why now? "I guess it's the only solution," I said.

My father leaned forward. He still looked sweaty and exhausted, even now that a cigarette was in his hand. "You don't think she'll be terrified, like that woman we saw?"

I figured I might as well be honest, since that's what he seemed to want. "Yeah, I think she will be," I said.

"Never get old," my father said, getting up to pay the check. "That's the answer."

"The alternative isn't that appealing," I said.

"No, it isn't," my father said. "Is it?"

CHAPTER FOURTEEN

We drove from the bar to Central Park, where Kaylo was in the play-off of his team's soccer game. My parents entered him in an after-school soccer program because they thought he wasn't that aggressive or interested in sports. Neither was I, but I guess they realize he's their last chance. Neither of them is at all athletic, so you'd figure it's just genes and why worry about it? But I don't have kids, so what do I know?

My mother was in the bleachers with a small group of other parents and some younger kids. Kaylo's team, the Eagles, were in green. The other team, the Hawks, were in blue. "So how'd it go?" my mother asked, turning to face us.

"We'll talk about it later," Dad said. He sat down next to her.

"The score is eight to nothing, the other side's favor," Mom said.

"*Ten* to nothing," said Kaylo's best friend, Wade. He was sitting disconsolately in the bleachers, his face in his hands.

"How come you're not playing, Wade?" I asked. He's a skinny little kid like Kaylo, but he wears glasses and is covered with freckles.

"I twisted my stupid ankle last week," he said.

124

"How's Kaylo doing?"

"Terribly . . . as usual." Wade likes Kaylo, but he's pretty unsparing in his judgments. "Kaylo hates to win, he *loves* losing."

"Isn't it just that he doesn't care so much if he loses?" I suggested.

"No," Wade said. "He hates winning! If our side wins, he says, 'Oh, bother.' "

The game was a little like the croquet game in *Alice in Wonderland* with hedgehogs as balls and flamingos as bats. No one seemed to quite know which direction they were supposed to be running in. A lot of kids ran ferociously down the field, but when they reached the ball they just stood there. I could see Wade's point about Kaylo. If you saw his face, it was clear that mentally he was somewhere else. It reminded me of those T-shirts that said: I'D RATHER BE HOME WRITING MY NOVEL. Kaylo's should have said: I'D RATHER BE HOME STUDYING DINOSAURS.

He waved at us and when the game ended, he trotted cheerfully over to where we were sitting. "Why're you looking so cheerful?" Wade said. "We lost."

"Well, can't win 'em all," Kaylo said.

"Yeah, but we haven't won *any*!" Wade exploded.

Kaylo shrugged. His face was bright pink. "Still, it's over anyhow."

"I thought you ran well," Mom said, handing him a can of Gatorade, which she had in her big straw bag.

"But he never kicks the ball," Wade said, exasperated. "The point of the game is to kick the ball."

"So? You twisted your ankle so you didn't kick the ball, either," Kaylo pointed out.

"You even let Sallie get past you!" Wade went on. "You just *stood* there."

"Hey, Wade, want to come back with us for dinner?" Kaylo said. For some reason none of this bothers him. Wade's his best friend and sports don't seem to him anything worth getting all upset about. And Wade, I think, admires Kaylo's vast knowledge about dinosaurs. "Mom said she'd take us to McDonald's. You want to come, too?" he asked me.

"Sure," I said. "Why not?"

"I thought you might have a date," Kaylo said. He gave Wade a nudge. "He goes out with *girls*." They both doubled over with laughter at the idea.

"Well, I'd better get home and take over with Granny," my father said. "See you later, kids."

"Sam, tell us how it went," my mother said. "Did you sign her up? Can she go right away?"

My father looked sweaty and harassed. "I don't know if it's the right place. There was something very disturbing about the way they treated some of the patients."

My mother looked like she was going to explode. "But the best places you have to sign up for years ahead, when you're *our* age practically. You *know* that."

"Okay, I know that!" my father yelled. "I know a lot of things. I'm trying to work out a solution that — "

"Yes, but *when*?" my mother interrupted. "This

126

can go on till she's driven us all into our graves! I just can't take it anymore."

"Well, I can't take your yammering on about it," my father said. "Leave me alone! It's my mother. I'm not just going to dump her in some hellhole and let her rot."

My mother turned away. "You're being absurdly melodramatic. And you happen to have a family. If we don't count more than her, why don't the two of you go off and live on some little desert island somewhere?"

"Maybe we will," my father said. He stormed off.

There was a dead silence. Kaylo and Wade had been horsing around some distance away and had missed the whole interchange. I looked at my mother. She looked like she was about to cry. She looked up at me, her eyes wet. "Why can't he understand?" she asked me. "Why is he so stubborn?"

"I guess, well, like he said, it's his mother." I tried to smile. "If it was you, I'd probably feel the same way."

At that my mother burst into tears. I sat there, patting her helplessly. "Hey, Mom, it'll be okay," I whispered. "Dad'll work something out." God, I felt rotten.

At that moment Kaylo and Wade came tearing up. "I thought we were going to McDonald's," Kaylo said. "We're starving."

"Yeah, we could eat a horse," Wade said. "We could eat a hundred horseburgers!"

"With ketchup!" Kaylo screamed, as though this

were the funniest exchange on earth.

My mother pulled herself together and drove us all uptown to McDonald's where Wade and Kaylo and I had burgers and fries and chocolate shakes. Mom asked me, "How did it go?"

"How did *what* go?" Kaylo asked. He had a dab of ketchup on his nose.

"Daddy and Charles were looking at nursing homes for Grandma," Mom said.

"But she's not a nurse!" Kaylo said. He slurped up the remains of his shake.

"She needs a place where people can look after her, trained people," Mom said. "Daddy wants to make sure it's a good place."

"Why can't she stay with us?" Kaylo said. "Josie can look after her."

Mom was beginning to look irritated. "Because that's not Josie's job, Kaylo. Josie has to clean the house and cook and pick you up at lessons. She has a lot to do. And she's not a trained nurse. Besides, you said Grandma was scaring you, the way she goes around at night, writing in your closet."

"Yeah, that was weird." Kaylo described to Wade how my grandmother had written in his closet with a green magic marker. "She said she was writing the story of her life."

"I don't even have a grandmother," Wade said. "They're all dead. I never even had one to begin with." He looked glum. "They're supposed to get you presents, aren't they?"

"Sometimes," Kaylo said. "You can't count on it, though."

CHAPTER FIFTEEN

My father called Ms. Delisio back a week or so later to find out when there would be room for my grandmother in the home. She told him that there would be a bed in a week to ten days. I think my father had expected it would take longer than that, but I guess someone had popped off just around the time we were there.

"Granny," my father said one night at dinner, "remember the place where you and Grandpa used to live in Florida?"

My grandmother shook her head with that trembling gesture she gets. "It was a terrible place," she said. "They stole everything! They took Abe's ties, all of them."

My father went on imperturbably. He'd had a few glasses of wine. "Remember all the nice friends you had there? Mrs. Heppenheimer? Mr. Green?"

"I remember." My grandmother looked at my father expectantly.

"Well, Charles and I were taking a drive in the country and we found a lovely place, much like that one but even nicer, and we thought you might like to go there for a little visit. A change of scene."

"To Florida?" My grandmother looked anxious.

"No, to a nice hotel not far from here where I

could visit you every day, where there are nice activities, Ping-Pong, painting. . . . It wouldn't be boring the way it is around here."

My grandmother shrugged. "It's boring everywhere. When you get old, it's boring."

"Well, this is a place especially designed for elderly people that has all kinds of things they might enjoy doing. I thought perhaps tomorrow you and I might drive up and take a look at it."

I figured I might as well help my father out since my mother wasn't saying anything. "It was a really nice place, Granny," I said. "I wish there was a place like that for people my age." There is: prison.

"You're going there, too?" my grandmother said, puzzled.

"No, I just went to look at it with Dad — to see what it was like."

"If I don't like it, can I come back here?" My grandmother's voice started to tremble.

"Of course," my father said. "Right away."

At that moment my mother said, "But Sam, you can't get a feeling of what a place is like right away. Gustel should stay at least a week or two to see how she likes it."

My father just waved his hand as though to tell my mother to be quiet. "After dinner we'll pack a few things, just a few nice dresses and some nice jewelry."

"It's all gone!" my grandmother cried. "My jewelry and dresses are all gone."

"No, you still have a lot of beautiful dresses. Remember the blue dress I got you last year for your birthday? You can take that."

130

My grandmother frowned. "No, I don't remember. What birthday was that?"

"You were eighty-one," my father said. "And we went to a lovely French restaurant and had champagne."

"I'm eighty-one?" my grandmother said, amazed.

"Yes, but you don't look a day over seventy," Dad said.

My grandmother looked around at all of us. "Imagine!" she said. "I thought I was — I don't *know* what. Seventy-five, maybe. Are you sure?"

"You don't act eighty-one or look eighty-one," my father said, "but you are."

My grandmother looked bemused. "Maybe that's why — Everything seems different. I wondered why. . . ." She got that lost, misty look. "I didn't used to be like this."

My father helped my grandmother up from her chair. "We'll just pack a few things," he said.

"I feel so tired," my grandmother said. "I'm too tired to pack."

"I'll pack," Dad said. "You just lie down and I'll hold the dresses up and you'll tell me what to pack." They went inside to my grandmother's room.

Kaylo was already in bed. My mother looked sad. "Well," she said, "I pray this will work out."

I went into my room and tried to type up my core report on South Africa. I had good notes, but my mind wasn't on it. I managed to get it done, though, and then I just lay down on my bed and started daydreaming about Wendy. I gave her a slightly different personality. She was a little more the way she'd been that day before her mother came home, more soft and yielding. Maybe that's what she thinks, too. Maybe she thinks I act sarcastic and weird most of the time. It's true. I often do, even when I don't intend to. Nasty remarks just come popping out of my mouth. Still, she said she thought I was funny and that's something. Being able to make a girl laugh is important, especially when you look like me.

My door opened a crack. "Granny would like to say good-night to you," my father said.

That was odd, but I figured it was because maybe in the morning I'd rush off to school and she would be at the nursing home by the time I got back. I went into her room. I saw the suitcase on the chair. "Hi, Granny," I said.

My father had tucked her in. She looked tiny in the bed, with just her head peeping over the covers. "Good-night, Charles," she said.

I had taken the shell I'd been saving for her from my room. "I thought you might want to take this along," I said. I set it down on top of the suitcase. "Granny found that on the beach," I explained to my father.

"What a beautiful shell," he said sadly, touching it gently and then setting it down again. I never forgot for the rest of my life the way my father said that.

I bent down and kissed my grandmother. I suppose I should have said something about how it had been nice having her stay at our apartment, but I didn't. "Sleep well," I said.

"Sweet dreams," my grandmother called softly as I left the room.

"Sweet dreams," I called back.

I left my father standing near my grandmother's bed, the night light casting a soft glow in the room.

CHAPTER SIXTEEN

When I came home from school next day, Josie was in the kitchen, on the phone. She looked different. She still had her wig on, the dark curly one. The minute she hung up, she said, "They got over there all right. The doctor said to tell you not to worry."

"About what?"

"Your grandmother died . . . in her sleep. They just came and got the body."

I felt shaky. I went in and sat down on one of the kitchen chairs. "But she was going to that nursing home."

"Well, she isn't going anyhere now," Josie said. "Poor old thing. I reckon it's for the best."

"Why do you have your wig on?" I asked.

Josie looked embarrassed. "The funeral people . . . I wanted to look elegant, the way I should." She yanked it off and tossed it on the marble table.

"In her sleep?" I asked again. "She died in her sleep?"

"That's what the doctor said. Said he tried to wake her this morning and she was gone. That's the way I'd like to go, I tell you. The perfect way."

I don't know why it seemed strange to me. It

was no stranger than Kim's grandfather dying in his sleep. But I hadn't known him that well. And my grandmother I had seen and talked to just a few hours before. "I don't think she would have liked that home," I said. "It was horrible."

Josie came over and sat across from me. "Your daddy's real upset, boy. You be careful with him, do you hear me?"

"What do you mean, be careful?"

"I just mean . . . lay back, be quiet. He's in some kind of mood. I've never seen him like that."

I didn't get exactly what she meant. "You mean loud? Yelling?"

"I can't explain it, just not his true self. It takes some people that way. Some people they just go right on, same as they always did. Others it takes funny. They go a little bit crazy. But it doesn't last. It's just a temporary thing."

Oh God. My father — crazy? I hope not. "Could you give me an example?"

"Well, like you know how your father doesn't care much about the proper way of doing things. Look at him. Look at the way he dresses. So right after he called the funeral home, he came into the kitchen here where I was doing my usual morning routine and he says, 'What are you doing?' 'Just cleaning up, Doctor,' I says. Which was true. You know, all your and Kaylo's breakfast things. He yells, 'Get in there and clean up that room! It's a pig sty!'" Josie laughed bitterly. "Whose fault is that? He knows as well as I do if I ever went in there and tried to make some order out of chaos,

135

your granny would start in on, 'Don't touch this, don't touch that, the shvartza this, the shvartza that.' "

I thought of what my father had told me when we were in the bar about all his mother had done for him. "I guess he's really upset," I said. "If it hadn't been for her, he might never have been a doctor or anything. He really loved her."

Josie nodded. "And she really loved him. I'd be sitting here, peeling apples, and she'd come in and say, 'Where's the doctor?' 'Out,' I'd say. Then she'd go on with, 'He's a prince,' she'd say. 'That man is a great man. He's the greatest, kindest man that ever did live.' On and on . . . and *on*."

I was feeling incredibly morose. "I wonder if anyone will ever say that about me."

Josie gave me an amused glance. "Your wife."

"What wife?"

"The wife that you'll have some day."

"What? Are you marrying me off already? I'm just a child. Anyway, I thought you said marriage was the pits, that you were never happier than when Hobart left you."

Josie shook her head. "Boy, you don't know anything yet, do you? Sure, in some sense I'm happier 'cause I don't have to sit home worrying how he's out spending all my hard-earned money on some floozy or putting a down payment on some damn fool new car. But, no, in lots of ways I miss him. I get lonely."

"You do?" I was amazed to hear that. "What do you miss about him?"

"Well, I miss his loving, if you must know. That

man knew how, believe me. And let me tell you, boy, there are few men that do . . . or can."

"Really?" Jesus, this is awful. I thought everyone knew, once they got started. I thought it was just a question of getting started. "What's there to it?" I asked anxiously, biting my nails. "Give me some hints. Maybe I'm doing it all wrong with Wendy."

"Just go slow, that's all. And love her. Love her *right*. That's all there is to it. Don't they give you sex education at that fancy school of yours?"

I made a face. "It's all weird diagrams. They ought to have some sexy blonde woman come in and show us the ropes, some sex therapist."

Josie approached me threateningly. "No, they should *not*! You have your sweet little Wendy and that's all you need. You treat her right and you'll get whatever you want. But I mean right in *every way*. Do you get what I'm saying?"

"Sort of."

Suddenly Josie stood up. "Before your daddy comes back, you and me are going to have a drink because I want to tell you he is in a bad mood."

"You're not supposed to drink because of your liver, and I'm a minor," I reminded her.

Josie snorted. She took out a quart of milk and went into the dining room where my parents kept their liquor. She poured a healthy dollop of Kahlua into the milk. "Milk is good for you," she said, handing me a glass. "This'll soothe you. We got a rough day ahead, Master Charles."

I didn't notice what Josie meant so much until evening when my Aunt Rachel and her second husband, Uncle Thorpe, were due to arrive for dinner.

They were planning to stay the night and then go to the funeral with us the next day. "Why are they staying here?" my father asked my mother.

"Well, they're relatives, sweetie. And a hotel room seems so — "

"I can't stand that man!" my father barked.

I gathered by that he meant Uncle Thorpe. Uncle Thorpe is a six-foot-five Scandinavian who has white eyebrows and works for IBM. "You didn't like the first one, either . . . Sewell."

"He drank," my father said. "They both drink. Why can't she marry someone sober?"

"She loves them. I mean, she loved them sequentially. And Thorpe has been good to her. He's helped raise her kids."

My father, speaking of drinking, was finishing off a bottle of Côte du Rhone. "So where were they when mother got sick? Where was all that milk of human kindness then?"

"They were in Fairbanks, Alaska, and you didn't want your mother up there. They offered, and you said no."

"They offered, knowing I'd say no." Suddenly my father glared at me. "These are your closest relatives, Charles. I want you to dress right and act right. I don't want you looking like something that rolled out of an ash can. Do you understand me?"

"Sure." God, Josie sure hit the nail on the head. I wished I could have another Kahlua and milk.

"And I don't want anyone going into Gustel's room," my father said. "Is that clear?"

Kaylo had been eating quietly, seeming not to pay attention to any of this. "Is her ghost in there?"

138

"Ghosts don't exist," my father said.

"Is her ghost in my closet?" Kaylo went on.

My mother scooped Kaylo up on her lap. "We don't have any ghosts," she said. "We never did and we never will."

"Wade said if someone dies in your house, their ghost stays there forever."

"Wade is an idiot!" my father said. "I don't want to ever see him again!"

At that Kaylo burst into tears. My mother gave my father a stern glance and took Kaylo out of the room. Dad just sat there morosely, hardly seeming to notice I was present. I saw Josie hovering in the background. "Should I clear?" she asked in her professional voice. "Is everyone done?"

"I'll help you," I said, jumping up.

"You sit still, Charles," my father said. "Josie has a job and she's doing it." Josie and I exchanged a glance. She said with her eyes to sit still and don't rock the boat.

What if my father really goes crazy? What if he flips? Does that mean I'll be head of the family? Maybe Aunt Rachel and Uncle Thorpe can take me to Fairbanks, Alaska. I watched Josie timorously set down some bowls of chocolate pudding. My father took one look at his and left the table.

"Where's the Kahlua? I think I need another shot."

Josie giggled. "You just hang in there, Charles. You're going to be fine. I'm counting on you."

My Aunt Rachel and Uncle Thorpe and their daughter Mariel arrived an hour after dinner. My father didn't even come out to greet them, though it was his family. My mother had put Kaylo to bed

139

and Josie had gone home. Aunt Rachel looks like a female version of my father. She's four years younger, but chubby and messy-looking with frizzy gray-black hair and round rimless glasses. Uncle Thorpe is like something out of the Charles Addams series on TV. He speaks about one word every half century. They have one son, Beal, who's retarded and sequestered in some special school in Maine, and their nineteen-year-old daughter, Mariel, who's a junior at Yale. She's very tall and blonde like Uncle Thorpe, with the same white eyebrows and pale blue eyes. Somehow on her it looks good.

"I'm sorry Sam turned in early," my mother said. "He's taking this very hard."

"He adored mother," Aunt Rachel said. "And it was certainly mutual. I was so jealous of their relationship when I was little. You're sure this is all right? We could stay at a hotel."

Mom hugged her. "Don't be silly. We want you here. I've got the guest room set up and I thought, if Mariel doesn't mind, she could take the spare bed in Charles's room."

If Mariel doesn't mind! How about *me*? It's my room.

Aunt Rachel laughed. "Oh, Mariel doesn't mind. She's in a coed dorm at Yale. Where are you going to college, Charles?"

"Cornell."

I might have said the University of Southern Miami from her expression. "Mariel adores Yale. You should have considered it. She got accepted everywhere, but she thought Brown was too preppy and Princeton too snobby and Harvard too . . . something."

Mariel just gave her mother that familiar shut-up-and-die expression. "Charles's room is fine," she said coolly, like: I'll sleep in a zoo as long as they sedate the animals.

"There's a sleeper couch in the dining room," I pointed out ungenerously.

"But then she wouldn't have her own bathroom," Mom said. She gave everyone drinks. Mariel had a Scotch on the rocks. I was impressed. I thought it might look strange if I asked for Kahlua and milk, so I just had ginger ale.

"This was so sudden," Aunt Rachel said. "She was fine, wasn't she?"

"No, she was deteriorating every day," Mom said. "It was really very, very difficult. I think that accounts for Charles's, I mean Sam's reaction now."

Aunt Rachel was nursing her vermouth. "Wasn't that just mental, though?"

"Oh, it was everything," Mom said, sighing. "It's really just as well this happened when it did. She was wandering around, not knowing where she was, scaring Kaylo. It was frightening."

Mariel and I sat silently, not taking part in the conversation. Mariel's my only cousin, unless you count Beal whom I hardly ever see. Mom's an only child. But since Mariel's always lived in Alaska and since Dad never seemed that close to Aunt Rachel, we don't have much of a relationship. I frankly doubt we would, even if we weren't related. I think the blood of the Vikings runs in her veins.

141

"Charles, you've had a hard day," my mother said. "Why don't you and Mariel turn in?" It was eleven.

I thought Mariel would make some crack about how she wasn't just a kid, but she silently followed me. She didn't make a whole big deal about getting undressed or getting ready for bed. Maybe that comes from living in a coed dorm. Or maybe she thinks I'm such a twerp it doesn't much matter if I see her naked or what. I didn't. She wears a black undershirt and bikini underpants to bed, an outfit which, if Wendy were in them, would be exciting. "Hey, have you got anything?" she whispered, once we were in our respective beds, with the lights out.

"Any what?"

"Stuff to knock me out. I'm wired."

Dad gives me Dalmane for insomnia as well as Valium. He says to alternate so I don't become addicted. I offered her the choice. "Wow, great. Can he get anything?"

"I guess."

She took two Valium. "Lucky you."

"Lucky to have insomnia?"

"Lucky to have a free drug supply right in your own house and an understanding father."

"He's not supporting a habit," I said sarcastically. "This is just to help me sleep if I feel tense."

"Sure," Mariel said in her gravelly, flat voice. "I thought in New York everyone was on something."

"Not everyone." She always makes me feel this way. Like if I'd said everyone in New York *was* on something, she'd have made some knowing remarks to imply we were all druggies.

We lay in silence for a while.

"How about for sex?" Mariel asked.

"What about it?"

"You just do it cold?"

I laughed. "I don't do it, period. I'm saving myself for my future wife, or husband, whichever comes along."

Mariel laughed, too. She has a sexy laugh or maybe it was just the circumstance of our being alone in the dark room, her in her black underwear. "You're kidding! You're a virgin?"

"Yup." Why was I telling her the truth? This wasn't a college interview. I'm quick-witted, I could have invented a million girls.

"God, that's so sweet. You have a girl friend and she's one, too, and you're, like, waiting."

"Not exactly."

"That's so sweet!" Mariel exclaimed, as though I hadn't just denied what she'd said. "You're so adorable, Charles! What do you do, like, just pet to orgasm or what?"

"Not even that."

"You're putting me on."

"Nope."

"So, what do you do?" She leaned forward, as though hoping it was something kinky.

"Well, we just kiss, basically, and maybe a little bit more."

Mariel laughed again. "God, the girls are going to love you at Cornell! They're going to eat you up alive! Hey, how come you didn't apply to Yale or Harvard?"

"My grades were erratic. I'm not a very good student."

"Well, anyway, the girls'll love you." She was silent. For a moment I thought she'd fallen asleep. "Grandma was sweet," she said in a wistful voice. "I remember how we used to visit her in Florida, how we used to collect shells on the seashore."

I thought of the shell I'd given Granny to take to the home. I wondered what happened to it.

CHAPTER SEVENTEEN

The funeral consisted of just the seven of us: me, Mariel, my aunt and uncle, my parents, and Kaylo. My grandmother was in a closed casket. There was no speech. We took two cars out to the cemetery somewhere in New Jersey. I think my father was drunk. Or at least he hardly spoke at all, and when he did, it was very slowly, as though English wasn't his native language. After the funeral he went off to work, saying good-bye briefly to my aunt and uncle. He said he hoped to see them again and Aunt Rachel hugged him, said to call any time he wanted to talk.

My aunt and uncle said they wanted to go to the Museum of Modern Art that afternoon. Mom said she would go with them. Kaylo was at a friend's house. Kim and Wendy both called a couple of times and I told them I'd be in school the next day. As my mother was about to leave, she came into the kitchen where Mariel and I were sitting with Josie, having Kahlua and milk. "Josie, I just wanted to say, if there's anything of Gustel's you'd like, any clothes or hats or whatever, please help yourself. I'm having everything taken away by the thrift shop tomorrow. Same with you, Mariel. Some of

145

the things are in excellent condition. She hardly wore them.''

What a ghoulish idea! I thought for sure Mariel and Josie would say no way, but to my surprise, after their drinks they both trooped into grandmother's room and began going through all her stuff. You could say, what's the difference between buying something in a thrift shop and just getting it straight, but it seemed ghoulish to me. Of course I couldn't fit into any of my grandmother's stuff anyway, so I just went in to see how they looked. The blinds were all drawn up and the room was flooded with light. The windows were opened. It still seemed to me that the room smelled of my grandmother, though. My mother had put all the clothes out on the bed or in boxes. There were shoes, hats, coats.

Mariel loved the hats. Some were those old-fashioned kind with veils. I don't remember ever seeing my grandmother wear them. "Oh, I love them,'' Mariel said. "Don't I look incredibly sexy? Wait till Blake sees me!''

"You try one on,'' I told Josie, who'd mainly been watching.

"No, I'm not the hat type. I don't like hats.''

Mariel tossed Josie a fur stole. "How about that?''

Josie draped the stole around her shoulders. She looked at herself in the mirror. "What do you think?''

"You look sensational,'' Mariel said. "It goes great with your hair!'' She meant Josie's real hair. She didn't have her wig on.

"Well, they did kill a whole bunch of innocent

146

minks to get that stole," I couldn't help pointing out.

"Yeah, but it's over," Mariel said, trying on another hat. "So, what difference does it make now? Anyhow, I heard minks are cruel, vicious little animals and they're only bred to be killed, so what's the difference?"

Josie was stroking the fur. It was a reddish brown color, like her real hair. "I do look kind of foxy," she said with a half smile.

"Minky, you mean," I said. "Yeah, take it, Josie. Maybe Willie'll give you another chance."

"Who's Willie?" Mariel asked, flirting with herself in front of the mirror.

"Her ex-boyfriend," I explained.

Josie shot me an exasperated glance. "Ex-nothing! We went out once."

Mariel was in her black bra and slip and bare feet. She began rummaging through my grandmother's shoes. When my grandmother was younger, up till she was seventy or so, she always wore high heels when she went out, those toeless kind you see in forties movies. "Black guys are something else," Mariel said, trying to fit her foot into one of my grandmother's shoes. "I went out with this black guy on campus, Lucius, and he was good, and, God, did he know it! Talk about conceited! Finally, he told me he thought he was betraying his race to date white girls. I said, 'Lucius, just because God or whoever or whatever tossed a little more brown pigment into you and a little less brown pigment into me, what's that have to do with betraying anybody or anything?' He wouldn't listen."

"Willie isn't black," I said, admiring Mariel's legs in the high-heeled sandals.

"Who's Willie?" Mariel asked, admiring her own legs.

God, she has the attention span of a gnat! How did she get into Yale? I was going to say, "Josie's ex-boyfriend," but I was afraid then we'd have to repeat the whole conversation, so I just said, "Forget it."

"I never was prejudiced," Josie said. She was in the bathroom trying something on. "But black men, some of them, they only like white women. That's what gets me."

"Was Hobart like that?" I asked.

"No, Hobart had every other fault you could name, just not that one."

Just as Mariel was kicking off one pair of shoes and trying on another, Josie came out of the bathroom. She was wearing one of my grandmother's bright green silk dresses. I never thought of Josie and my grandmother as the same size, but whereas the dress would've hung on Granny, on Josie it fit just right. I whistled.

Josie walked self-consciously across the room over to the mirror and inspected herself. "It's too short," she said.

Mariel looked at her, her hands on her hips. "Not by much. Maybe an inch or two. Wait till your boyfriend sees that!"

"I don't have one," Josie said glumly.

"You will," Mariel said. "That fits you perfectly. And the green is great with your hair. How come

148

you don't have a boyfriend? Are you still married?"

"Lord no," Josie said. "Married! I haven't seen Hobart B. Eubanks in seven years."

"Are you still pining for him?"

"Pining! No, men aren't worth pining over, that's for sure." Josie went over and held another dress up in front of her.

"Yeah, but sometimes . . ." Mariel said. She sat down and held a shoe in one hand. "They can sure get under your skin, some of them. Even the worst ones."

"*Especially* the worst ones," Josie said darkly.

I felt I ought to be defending my sex. "How about women? They're not cruel? They don't rip you to shreds just for the fun of it, undermine your ego?"

"Oh Charles, don't be a baby!" Mariel said.

Josie came over and ruffled my hair affectionately. "He *is* a baby, but he's sweet. He's my sweet baby."

I got up and started to do a soft-shoe dance across the room. "He's my sweet baby, yessir, my sweet baby."

Just then the door was flung open. It was my father. "What in God's name is going on in here?" he yelled.

There was a moment of dead silence. Finally Mariel spoke in a whispery little voice. "Dr. Goldberg, Aunt Megan said we could try on some of Granny's clothes before the Goodwill people come to take them away."

Dad strode into the room. He began flinging the clothes on the floor. "Don't you have any money for clothes, Mariel? Josie? Here, take some money!

Go to Saks! Go to Bonwit's!" He threw a whole heap of ten-dollar bills at them. Then he noticed me. "What are *you* in here for?"

"He was helping us decide what we looked good in," Mariel said, looking scared.

"What the hell does he know?" my father screamed. "He doesn't know a goddamn thing." Then suddenly he bent over and started to sob. His whole body shook. He buried his face in his hands.

I felt petrified. But Josie went over and put her arms around my father. "Dr. Goldberg, you're just tired, that's all you are. You come inside with me and lie down and I'll fix you some good soothing tea. You just come right along." I was sure my father would shake Josie off in a fury, but he followed her quietly out of the room, holding onto her arm, like he was an old man.

After they'd left, Mariel looked at me. "Gee, I'm sorry. I never would've tried anything on if Aunt Megan hadn't. . . ."

I began folding up the dresses my father had scattered around the room. "It's okay," I said. "Take whatever you want. Just put them in a shopping bag and go."

Quietly Mariel began stuffing things into a large shopping bag. "I hope he'll be all right," she said. "Do you think he will be?"

"I hope so," I said.

150

CHAPTER EIGHTEEN

My father did seem all right, gradually, in the months after my grandmother's death. Mom convinced him to take a long vacation and they went to the south of France for three months. Kaylo was in summer camp and I had a job at McDonald's so I don't know exactly what those three months were like for them, but by the time they returned in the fall, my father seemed like his own self. He still smoked all the time and started forgetting to put out cigarettes, so that there were quite a few burned places on end tables around the apartment. He kept on drinking and eating more than he should have. But otherwise he seemed the same as he'd always been.

I went away to college, to Cornell. Then the Sunday before Thanksgiving vacation, I came into my dorm room from the library. The phone was ringing. It was my mother. She said my father had lost consciousness and died an hour before. "I don't think he suffered," she said, her voice shaky. "He just passed out."

Actually, it wasn't as though my father was in wonderful shape, even for someone in his fifties. He never stopped smoking. He used to carry a little scissors around and take a few puffs of a cigarette, then clip the cigarette off. But he breathed heavily and when the doctor told him he was in terrible condition, he'd say, "The world's in terrible shape and it's not doing anything about it. Why should I?"

I sat in the easy chair in my room and listened to my mother describe how my father had died. I didn't feel anything. Or, rather, when she said, "Your father died," I felt something I can't exactly describe, a quick wave of horror or disbelief, which passed so fast it was as though it hadn't happened. But when she was describing his death, I felt perfectly calm and was only aware of wanting to comfort her and make her feel better.

"You know how he's been having these dizzy spells?" she said. "But he wouldn't see the doctor. Finally I said, 'Just let George take a look at you.' " George is an internist, my father's oldest friend. "George came over and said, 'He should go to the hospital for a checkup.' But you know Sam. He wouldn't. He just said George was an alarmist, that the dizzy spells were due to the heat. This morning we both woke up late and he got up and said, 'God, I feel awful, Megan. Could you get me a cup of coffee?' I said sure and I went into the kitchen. The coffee was already made on that new Japanese machine we got for Christmas. I poured a cup and carried it back to the bedroom. When I got there, he was lying on the floor. I went over and held him in my arms. He seemed only half conscious. 'Can you hear me?' I asked him, and he murmured, 'Yes.' I said, 'I have to call the hospital.' I tried to reach for the phone without letting go of him, and I did.

I called for an ambulance, and then I just sat there on the floor with him in my arms. I asked if he wanted anything, and he said no. I asked if he was feeling any pain and he said no. He felt cool and sweaty at the same time. I just sat there, Charles. It seemed like hours and hours. I knew he was dying. He was dying right then, while I held him. I could feel it! And then the ambulance came and they took him away. They said it was too late, but they took him anyway. I called George and he met me at the hospital." My mother's voice was beginning to shake more now. "George said there wasn't anything I could've done. He said I did the right thing."

"You did, Mom," I said. "You know you did."

"Why didn't I get him to the hospital the week before the way George said? Why didn't I insist?" She was crying.

"He wouldn't have gone," I said. "He was like that."

"Why was he like that?" my mother said. "Why?"

"I don't know."

"He hated hospitals. He said they were like prisons. Maybe it's just as well he died this way, at home, with me right there. . . . Oh Charles!"

I could hear her crying over the phone. "Mom, listen, I'll take the plane and be there in a couple of hours. It's ten now. I'll be there by early afternoon."

"Can you make it? Do you have classes?"

"It's almost Thanksgiving. I'll have my roommate tell my professors. Hold on, okay? Take a Valium."

My mother sighed. "I took two already."

My roommate, Hal, isn't someone I'm that close to. We just share this suite with a connecting living room. I wrote him a note, telling him where I'd gone and why. All the time I was writing the note and packing, I still felt very calm, almost unnaturally calm. I watched my hand form the letters and it seemed to me my handwriting was very neat and even. I didn't pack much. It was November, but we'd been having mild weather and I figured it would be warmer in New York.

On the plane, I began wondering if I should have called Kim. He's still my best friend, even though he's at Harvard. Wendy's there, too. Both of them have let their music and dance slide. He's premed and she's a history major. Strangely, or maybe not, they're going together. He said it started because they were both shy and didn't have much to talk about except me. Then, as they say, one thing led to another, and now it's pretty serious. They may even get married after graduation. That makes sense. They were both serious people even back in high school. I guess I was the comic relief. When the three of us get together, I can still make them laugh, but I get the feeling that when they're alone, they say how infantile I am and how little I've changed. In a way that's true. I'll probably still be cutting up and making asinine remarks even when I'm eighty and my wife is beating me over the head with her cane. But inside I've changed.

Outside I've changed a little, too. I run. Actually, it's more very fast walking; it's an art in itself. You really burn up the calories. I wouldn't say I'm as slim as a wraith, but I'm not the old pulpy hulk I used to be. Despite these outward changes — my skin has cleared up, too — I feel pretty much the same. I don't spend a lot of time gazing into mirrors. When I do catch sight of myself though, I feel pleasantly surprised.

On the plane I sat next to a business executive-type girl with an attaché case. She had a double Scotch and explained it was because she was afraid of flying. I had one, too, and explained it was because my father had just died. "My mother's a widow now," I said. My words sounded slow and almost profound. "She's on her own."

"My mother's been a widow forever," the girl said. She looked just a little like my cousin, Mariel. "But she has a boyfriend. He's just had a lot of trouble getting a divorce."

"My mother'll never have a boyfriend," I said, horrified. "She's not like that."

The girl, Carlyle Hunt, said she'd thought the same about her mother. "They surprise you. They have needs, just like us."

My mind veered off to my mother and her possible sexual needs, but that was a taboo subject so it veered back to Carlyle Hunt and her implication that she had sexual needs. Or did she just mean companionship? "Are you talking about sex?" I asked, motioning to the stewardess for another drink.

"Was I?" asked Carlyle Hunt. "I thought we were talking about our mothers being widows."

"We were talking about their needs," I said, "about why they have boyfriends."

"Oh . . . that." Carlyle gazed beyond me outside the window, though there wasn't much to see. "In

Mother's case, it's more to have someone to read aloud to in the evening and worry about me and fix the furnace when it breaks down."

"So, you think for her the sex part is basically irrelevant?"

Carlyle blushed. "They sleep without any clothes on, so what can I tell you?"

"That sounds incriminating." It seemed obscene to be talking about sex a few hours after my father's death. Then I remembered all his worries about me, about my lack of experience. At least I've lost my virginity by now. He could die without having to worry about that.

The conversation with Carlyle Hunt could have made me horny, under other circumstances, except I hate girls with blonde hair and attaché cases who have names like hotels. Also, I have a girl friend. My father hadn't met her yet; neither had my mother. We've just been, as it were, going together, for six weeks. I was going to bring her home over Christmas. Maybe I still will.

In the cab on the way to our apartment, I tried to think about my father. When I tried to think about him, I couldn't. He'd appear and vanish. I'd remember bits and pieces of him — his nose or trembling hands as he reached for his pack of cigarettes before he got out of bed, his leaning back in his Naugahyde reclining chair late at night when I'd have insomnia (which I still have), listening to Brahms and reading Boswell's diaries. I got out of the cab and gave my suitcase to the doorman, Jules.

When I got home, I found my mother in my father's study. "Everything's such a mess," she cried.

156

"He was so untidy. Ingram is coming and I don't know where anything is."

My mother, apart from seeming distraught, looked the same, in a blue cotton dress, her hair fluffed out. I put my arms around her and hugged her. She stood there, clinging to me. "Kaylo's at Wade's house. He slept there last night. His parents are telling him and sending him home by cab. I wanted to wait till you got here. Should I have done that? Maybe I should have let him finish out the day with them."

"You did the right thing," I said.

"It was this morning!" my mother cried. "It was less than five hours ago."

"He wasn't in good shape, though," I said. "You knew that."

"I knew it, but I thought he'd live forever. Isn't that silly? All I ever worried about was who he'd marry when I died. I was worried about all those silly women like Portia who would descend on him. Sam was such a fool about women."

What a strange remark. To me my father had always seemed so urbane and courtly with women. "I guess I didn't expect it, either," I admitted.

"It's better," my mother said. "What's the good of going around worrying every single second? He said life wasn't worth living without cigarettes. He knew he was in bad shape. But I think . . . I think he had a good life, don't you?"

I nodded.

"He'd seen you pull yourself together; he was so proud of Kaylo. I think I was a good wife to him. I tried to be, anyway." She faltered again.

157

Lots of times in my life I've been unable to figure out what my mother wanted or expected of me. This was easy. She wanted comfort and reassurance. I gave it to her. It made it easier for me, too. It gave me something to do. When Kaylo came home from Wade's house, we were still in the living room, trying to sort through my father's insurance papers. Kaylo rushed right into the room and into Mom's arms, crying. "Where is he?" he said.

"They took the body away," my mother said. It sounded strange the way it was no longer "Daddy" or "your father," just "the body."

"But I wanted to see him," Kaylo cried. "I never said good-bye to him or anything."

Kaylo has grown some but, at eleven, he's still small for his age and on the skinny side. Mom says he has a girl friend now, Andrea, who's in his piano class. At least they produced one moderately normal-seeming son, in looks and reactions. I was touched at the way Kaylo cried so openly and ran to Mom, even though he's almost a teenager now. He's never been afraid to show what he feels. I'll always be afraid. "Did you see him?" he asked me.

"No, I just arrived about an hour ago."

At that Kaylo came over and hugged me, too. "I feel terrible," he said.

"We all do," I said inadequately.

Suddenly Kaylo became angry. "He wouldn't stop smoking! That was so stupid. Why didn't he?"

My mother sighed. "People can't always stop doing things, even though they know they're bad for them," she said.

"Then it's his own fault he died," Kaylo said. "I hate him!" He started to cry again.

Mom held Kaylo and over his head looked at me with a half smile, the way she used to look at Dad, as though we were the two adults now. "Daddy was very proud of both of you," she said. "We were just talking about that last night, how well you've both turned out."

Kaylo and I looked at each other. Did Dad really think that? Or was it just Mom's illusion? "You got thin," Kaylo said, looking at me.

"Yeah, girls are after me in droves," I said dryly.

"Do you have a girl friend?"

"Sort of." I didn't feel like talking about that now.

Kaylo sat down in Dad's reclining chair. "What do we do now?"

"We wait for the lawyer to come," my mother said, "and he'll try and sort through all these papers. Boys, you don't have to hang around inside with me. Why don't you go for a walk? It's such a lovely day."

Kaylo looked at me uncomfortably. "Do you want to?"

"Sure." I glanced at my mother. "You're sure you don't want me around when he comes?"

"Oh darling, he won't be here for hours. Just be back in time for dinner."

Kaylo and I walked into the park near the Metropolitan Museum. I thought of the day we had had the picnic, Grandma peeing on the grass, Kaylo doing his dance, Mrs. Wolfe in her floppy hat,

Wendy. I still feel a pang about Wendy, like I somehow fucked up with her, although I don't know in what way and I'm not sure I'd handle it differently if I had it to do over. I guess I need someone who, even when I'm saying stupid or insensitive things, can see through to what I really mean. Wendy was always getting hurt and she'd look at me with her big baleful eyes. Kim is a lot better for her. I'm not even jealous. In fact, if I'm jealous of anything it's that he spends so much time with her, just the way he used to with me. Maybe if Lorraine and I really click, I won't mind so much.

"How's it going with Andrea?" I asked Kaylo.

"Okay." He looked as though he didn't get my question. "She likes me, I like her, no problems."

How can he be eleven and be so cool about everything? "Don't you ever have fights, get on each other's nerves?"

"Sure. Sometimes."

For some reason it got me angry, how damn calm he was, the same day Dad had died. "So, you going to marry her?" I said, to needle him.

"Maybe." It's hard to needle Kaylo.

I felt like a jerk for wanting to. I had this image of Dad watching us walking along, listening to our conversation. "How's living at home been with just Mom and Dad?" I said. "I mean, with me off to college. Is it different?"

"Different from what?"

"From when I was there. I mean, did you like having them pay all that attention to you?"

"They didn't pay that much attention to me, no more than before. At least not that I noticed." He hesitated. "Dad never talked to me that much. He talked more to you or Mom."

He said that unbitterly, just as a fact. "He didn't talk much to me, either," I said.

"What I mean is," Kaylo went on, "I didn't feel like I knew him that well. That's a weird thing to say about your father, but I just didn't."

"Yeah." I knew what he meant. But in some way I did feel I knew Dad fairly well, though if you were to ask me a lot of facts about him, what his opinions were on this or that, I couldn't say. Our best talks were late at night, when we both had insomnia. Then it was like it was just the two of us, floating around in the dark, like two fishes. He didn't seem like he felt he had to act like a father, and I didn't feel like I had to act like a son at those times. "Well, now it'll be just you and Mom."

"That's okay," Kaylo said. He looked up at me. "Do you figure she'll get married again?"

"I don't know. I can't imagine it. Can you?"

"No! Boy, she better not, not for a long time, anyway. She better not *ever*."

It's true I still think of Mom and Dad, different as they were, as being one person. Momanddad. I can't imagine Mom "dating," starting to wear sexy clothes, or doing whatever women her age do when they're on the make. I've heard women sometimes marry their lawyers. When we got home I took a long look at Ingram Eisinger, our family lawyer. He and Mom had all Dad's papers spread out and were going over them. "Hi, Charles, hi, Kaylo," he said. I used to think he was gay, but he's married. Of course, I guess he could be both. Somehow he

161

doesn't seem Mom's type, but I realize all I know of her type is Dad.

When Ingram left, Mom said, "The funeral will be tomorrow at eleven."

"Did you call Aunt Rachel and Uncle Thorpe?"

She shook her head. "I'll tell them after it's over. Dad said he didn't want anyone but the immediate family. I even found it in writing among his papers. She handed me a lined yellow sheet, which said in ink:

> I, Samuel Michael Goldberg, being of sound mind and body, request that there be present at my funeral only my immediate family — my wife Megan, and my sons Charles and Kaylo. I want no flowers, no speeches, no ceremony of any kind, no memorial service, and no contributions to charity. May I rest in peace.

I smiled. "That makes it pretty clear."

My mother was beginning to look exhausted. "I'm going to lie down, Charles. We'll go out to eat later, all right?"

"Sure, that's fine with me."

"Oh, and Charles? Josie is coming in tomorrow. I thought she might come to the funeral, too. I think of her as immediate family, even though Sam didn't specifically mention her. Do you think he'd mind?"

I thought of something I'd once read that said everything that happens after the death of someone is for the survivors. "I don't think he'd mind," I said. I really don't.

CHAPTER NINETEEN

Sometime late in the afternoon Kim called. He'd found out about my father from Hal, my roommate. "Wendy and I were planning to fly in tomorrow for Thanksgiving," he said. "We'd like to see you. Is that okay?"

"Sure."

I felt tired myself, but when I tried lying down in my former room, I couldn't fall asleep. I say "former room" because Mom has turned it into a guest room. It's not that different. She just gave the desk away and put down a new bright green carpet and had the walls painted. Anyone would say it looks like a more attractive room now, but it doesn't seem like my room anymore. She let me keep some of my collections in the closet, like my shells.

Just because I had nothing better to do, I took down the shells and began going through them. Some of them are real beauties. There were the ones I'd collected with my grandmother on the beach in Florida, and some my parents brought back from their travels. Lorraine's birthday is in a week. I could give her a shell. And some perfume maybe. I realized I hadn't left word with her about my father. We've only been dating, or rather sleeping together and seeing each other exclusively, for six weeks. It's been an intense month, more like three years in some ways, but when sex is good, you spend so much time either doing it, thinking about it, or daydreaming about it that you sometimes forget to mention the basics like: I have an eleven-year-old brother, I used to be fat in high school, I hate creamed spinach.

I wonder if Mom will move. This apartment is so huge, all these winding hallways and closets. No wonder my grandmother used to feel lost in it. It's probably worth a fortune, too, not that money has ever been a major problem, but I suppose it could be now. I don't think Mom and Portia earn all that much from their catering service.

We had an early dinner, and all of us turned in as soon as we got home. Mom seemed sad and preoccupied. I didn't know if she was worrying about the future, life without Dad, about money, about whether she'd been a good wife, but I didn't feel I could ask. Kaylo didn't eat much, just shoved his food around his plate and acted a little spacy. Frankly, I think I was the most tuned in of the three of us, which wasn't saying much.

I didn't sleep all night. I'd left my Dalmane and Valium back at school, and by three I realized I just wasn't going to sleep, so I gave up on it. I went into Dad's study and sat there in his reclining chair. For some reason on an impulse I put that Brahms trio he liked so much on the phonograph. It was like a private memorial service, just the two of us. Rooms smell like the people who are in them most of the time. There was still a smell in the room that reminded me of Dad, not an unpleasant smell, partly the tobacco from his cigarettes. Why could he never give them up? Why did we both have insomnia?

I think I dozed off because the next thing I remember was Josie peeking into the room and shaking me. "Charles! What are you doing in here?"

I felt groggy. "Oh, I just . . . I couldn't sleep. What time is it?"

"It's eight in the morning." Sun was streaming in the dusty windows.

"The funeral's not till eleven."

"I know. But I figured your mother could use some help with the house, tidying up and what all."

I felt glad to see Josie, almost absurdly glad. "I guess I better shower and get ready. It's no big deal. Just us."

"I know. That's the way the doctor liked things. No frills."

I watched Josie go around the study, tidying up. She's gotten a little heavier, but she doesn't look any older to me. I guess I don't think of Josie as being any real age. It's funny to think that when she first came here to work for us she was just in her early twenties and Hobart used to pick her up every night in his Cadillac.

"So, how's life?" I asked her, stretching.

"Nothing special, same old stuff." She grinned. "Nothing like you."

"Me? You've got to be kidding."

"Big college boy. Even got thin on me. Girl friends."

"How do you know I have a girl friend?"

165

"Don't you?"

"I'll tell you about it later." I always knew Josie had extrasensory perception.

The four of us took a cab to the funeral parlor. Kaylo and I wore suits, but Josie and my mother just wore regular dresses, as though to obey my father's order that nothing be different than it would normally have been. We were ushered into a large room by an obsequious man who told us to wait until they were ready. My father's casket was in one corner of the room. It was closed.

"How come the casket is closed?" I asked in a low voice.

"I thought he'd prefer that," Mom said.

I guess what I did then was odd. I went over and, when no one was looking, I opened the casket and looked in. I was sorry I had. My father's body had started to decompose. I know if I'd seen him "laid out," made up the way they usually do with corpses, that would have bothered me, too. But this was awful. Luckily no one saw me.

Finally the funeral director appeared and said, if we were ready, we could get into the limousine to drive to the cemetery. It was a huge, long black car. Kaylo and my mother got in front. I sat in the back with Josie. What kind of conversation do you make on the way to a funeral? If you talk about the person who died, it seems false. If you talk about anything else, it seems frivolous. For some reason I was glad I was with Josie, someone who never pretends about anything, with whom I can always be myself.

For a long time, neither of us said anything. We

each just looked out the window. Finally, Josie said, "Here my Daddy's almost eighty and he isn't fit for anything but driving Mama crazy and getting dead drunk. And he'll probably outlive us all."

"Will you be upset when he dies?"

"I'm closer to my mama, always was." After a few moments, she turned to me with a half smile. "So tell me about this girl friend, Charles."

"She's a girl. What can I tell you?"

"Of course she's a girl! I know you're not one of those pansy types. What's her character?"

"Well, she's tall. She's going to be a lawyer. She's from San Francisco, and she's six months older than me."

Josie frowned. "A lawyer? One of those women's lib types, huh?"

"Right. My plan is one day she'll get elected to the Supreme Court and I'll stay at home, reading in a hammock and keeping an eye on our kids."

"Kids! You planning on kids already? It must be serious."

"No, we're not planning anything, really. We're just in love." I gave her what I hoped was a winning smile.

"Do you have her photo?"

Actually I did. I had a photo I'd taken last month of Lorraine in front of a big oak tree on campus, laughing because I'd just said something incomparably witty. I handed it to Josie. She stared at it. "Boy, this girl is black!"

"Is she? I thought the negative was just over-exposed."

Josie glared at me. "Haven't you learned anything yet? What are you doing with a black girl friend?"

"I told you, we're in love. What's wrong with that?"

"How about your mama? How's she going to take it? How about her folks? Have you thought of that?"

"Why are you so conventional all of a sudden? We're in love. You were the one who used to say if two people are in love, nothing else matters."

"I said such foolishness?"

"Something like that. You used to worry I wouldn't find anyone. I was too weird and sarcastic. Well, now you can rest easy. I did."

"I never said any such thing," Josie said indignantly. "You're just twisting my words. I just wanted you to shape up a little. If it hadn't been for me, I doubt you'd have taken more than two showers the whole time you were in high school."

"Maybe three," I agreed.

Josie gave me one of her piercing glances. "Does she treat you right?"

"She needles me, she keeps me in line, the way women are supposed to. She laughs at my jokes." Actually, when I tell a joke, Lorraine throws back her head and laughs so hard I get worried, though I'm also grateful. Then she says in her drawling voice, "Charles, you are impossible. . . ." Mom has this theory that women are attracted to men who are the opposite of their fathers. I'm certainly a prime case of that. Lorraine's father is tall and bald, voted for Reagan, and used to be a Marine sergeant. He'll probably have a heart attack when he meets me. Then neither of us will have fathers.

Josie was still staring at the photo as though she was going to have to identify Lorraine in a police lineup. "What are those funny shoes she has on?"

"They're track shoes. She's a runner. She's captain of the women's track team."

Josie snorted. "That's how come you got so thin, huh? Running after her?"

"No, she ran after *me*. You know how women always pursue men. We just lie there helplessly and let them have their way with us."

Josie turned to me. "Charles, I just want to know one thing. Are you treating her right?"

"Right? What's right? Sure I'm treating her right."

"You know what right is, boy. I don't have to explain."

"Yes, you do. Do you mean do I beat her or what? The answer to that is no because if I did, she'd sling me against the wall and I'd never get up again."

"I mean, do you make her feel good about herself . . . in every way? Now I do not have to spell that out for you. You're seventeen years old."

I gathered this meant sex. "I try my best." I looked at Lorraine's photo. "I love her. She's probably too good for me. What else can I tell you?"

"When do I get to meet her?"

"At Christmas. I was going to have Mom and Dad meet her, but I guess it'll just be Mom . . . and you." I smiled. "I've told her a lot about you."

Josie looked horrified. "You have? What have you told her?"

"Oh, just how cruel you were to me when I was

a mere slip of a child, how you got me on Kahlua and milk when I was still in the cradle."

Josie snorted. "Charles, you are something else. Seventeen years old and you haven't changed one whit."

"But think how awful you'd feel if I *had* changed." I grinned. "You love me just the way I am."

Josie looked embarrassed. "Huh!" was all she said.

In a strange way I think Dad would have liked this kind of nonceremony where all the amenities, almost, were disregarded. He would have hated a lot of important fellow pathologists standing around telling about what a great guy he was and what a contribution he'd made to medicine. He'd much rather Josie and I chewed the fat about Lorraine.

The four of us walked to the cemetery and stood while the casket was lowered into the ground. The sun had gone behind a cloud so it wasn't quite as hot as it had been. Kaylo was holding my mother's hand and trying not to cry. My mother's face had a grave, almost serene expression as though whatever she was feeling was too deep to be expressed in tears. I saw the tombstones of my grandparents just in back of my father's — plain granite slabs like his with their names and dates.

After the burial was over, my mother said, "Let's all just think of Sam in whatever way we want for a few minutes. I'm not going to say a prayer or a eulogy."

We all stood there. The sun came out and shone on the tombstone. I still felt as I had when I'd gotten my mother's phone call, as though part of me was under anesthesia, as though if someone had asked about my father I'd have said, "Oh, he's a pathologist." I thought of Lorraine tickling me in bed.

Then Mom turned to us and said, "I'd like to be here just a moment with him. Is that all right?"

Josie and I left her standing there and walked through the beautifully tended green grounds. Kaylo trailed behind, peering at gravestones. "It sure is beautiful here," Josie said. "Peaceful. I'd like this kind of place."

"To live in or be buried in?"

"Oh, I just meant. . . ." Josie gave me a shy kind of smile. "I used to have this fantasy if I was ever rich — don't tell me, I know I won't be, ever — how I'd buy some old house in the country in Virginia. The house wouldn't matter, just someplace comfortable. But it would have acres of land."

"What would you do with all that land?"

Josie smiled dreamily. "I'd have a huge garden. Fruit, vegetables, flowers, plum trees, you name it. And every morning while it was still cool, I'd get up and take care of my garden."

"What would you do the rest of the day?"

"Visit folks, play cards, walk, do some shopping, you know. And in the evening I'd have a meal just of what I'd planted in that garden, everything fresh, no meat except maybe if I caught some fish in my pond."

It sounded really nice. "Could I come visit?"

"Sure you could, Charles. You and whoever you married and your kids and Kaylo and your mama. You could all come." She laughed. "Only that's just a fantasy."

171

"Fantasies are good," I said. "You've got to have fantasies."

"You're right," Josie said. "You sure do."

After that we got back in the limousine and drove back to the city.

CHAPTER TWENTY

The next afternoon Kim and Wendy came over. They talked awhile with my mother and then Kim suggested we take a walk. My mother said she was feeling tired, but she added, "You go, Charles. It's such a lovely day."

We walked up to Ninetieth Street. Kim and Wendy held hands. I'm glad in a way they're so relaxed with me and with each other. Kim acts with Wendy the way I think she always wanted me to act. He's protective and kindly. I guess you could call it masculine, but it's not some macho trip. He clearly just sees her as fragile emotionally and wants to take care of her. Actually, Wendy's filled out a lot. I wouldn't say a talent scout would rush her to pose for a pin-up spread, but her collar bones don't stick out so much.

"I was thinking of your father today," Kim said. "I realize how much I owe him. I never would have wanted to be a doctor if it hadn't been for him. He used to talk about medicine as though it was so alive and interesting. It really made an impression on me."

That's strange. I don't remember my father ever talking about medicine to me. Maybe he tried and I didn't listen, or maybe it's just easier to talk to other people's fathers than to your own. "I think he liked being a doctor," I said. "I never could understand why."

Wendy looked shocked. "But you're helping other people get well."

"Not if you're a pathologist," I couldn't help pointing out.

"You're trying to understand disease, what goes wrong, so maybe the next time — " Kim looked self-conscious. "What I mean is, my own father always struck me as a businessman pure and simple. He wanted to make money and he has. But he never cared about abstractions. He didn't care about my music and he doesn't really understand why I want to be a doctor."

Wendy laughed. "My father doesn't understand anything! 'Dance in the living room, dance for your husband.' Remember, Charles?"

I feel a pang when Wendy looks at me so softly and forgivingly. Why should I? I didn't do anything that awful to her that needs forgiving. If it weren't for me, she wouldn't have met Kim or maybe wouldn't have gotten close to him. "Your father was a jerk," I agreed.

"It's funny, though," Wendy said. "I thought when Mom divorced him, she'd marry someone better, and the new one is just as much of a jerk. She just likes to be dominated by dumb men, I suppose."

"Sounds like ninety percent of the female population," I observed.

"Charles!" Wendy never could and never can tell when I'm joking. "What a terrible thing to say!"

174

"It explains Reagan," I said.

She almost involuntarily moved closer to Kim. "There are many exceptions," she said softly.

Just for the heck of it we decided to walk down to Diamond. "Is Kaylo liking it?" Kim asked.

"Yeah, he's still plugging away at the piano. He has a girl friend now."

Wendy laughed. "But he's so young!"

"They're doing everything earlier than we did. We were all socially backward."

"I was really a mess," Wendy agreed.

"I don't agree," Kim said. "I think we did things at the right time . . . for us. We were smart. We didn't rush into things we weren't ready for."

I sighed. "Not me. I was ready. I just couldn't find anyone to do it with." I glanced sideways at Wendy. "With a few seminotable exceptions."

Stiffly Wendy said, "Kim knows everything we did or didn't do, Charles, so don't try and make it into more than it was."

"Me? Never!"

We reached Diamond just as assembly was beginning. When we told the woman at the front desk we were former students, she said we could sit in the back. I've stopped my singing lessons, though I belong to the glee club and still like to sing. I guess what I never enjoyed was the performing part. Tuberosa used to tell us that all great singers hated performing, too, but I think what he meant was partly they hated it and partly they loved it, and only came to life when they were doing it. I thought of the time I'd sung "*Un'aura amorosa*" with my parents and my grandmother in the audience.

175

It was right after she'd come to live with us, before she'd begun going downhill.

Somehow, thinking of my grandmother made me start thinking of my father, and that got me depressed. It was Kim's remark about how inspiring my father had been when he talked about medicine, and how I never did talk to him about that, and now would never have the chance. I always felt my father disapproved of me in some way, though he claimed he didn't. At times I felt I reminded him of things about himself that he didn't like: lack of discipline, sloppiness, nervousness, awkwardness with people. Kaylo was and is more like Mom and I think he just found him charming.

After the assembly, as we were going out, Ms. Talbot, my singing teacher, spotted me. "Charles!" she exclaimed. "What a surprise. You must have Thanksgiving vacation."

I didn't want to mention about my father's death, so I just said yes. I introduced Wendy and Kim. I knew she didn't know them well because neither of them had taken singing. "How splendid to have three distinguished alumni back among us," she trilled. "What a treat! If you want to stop in my classes, please do. We meet at two-thirty in room six-oh-one."

None of us felt like staying any longer. We started giggling on the way out. "Three distinguished alumni," Wendy mocked.

"We'll distinguish ourselves," Kim said. "Only in other fields. I don't think what I learned was a waste, do you?"

"Oh no," Wendy said. She kissed him. "But I

was never really talented, like you. I never could have gone professional."

"Who knows if I could have?" Kim said. "It's a grueling life, so competitive."

They were going to Kim's house. I dropped them off by cab and continued on home.

That night I called Lorraine. "I'm sorry about your father," she said. "Why didn't you call me?"

"I did, but you were out," I lied. "And I felt — "

"Sure, I understand. Are you okay now?"

"Yeah. I feel numb more than anything."

"That's how it is. It takes a while to set in."

We were silent.

"I miss you," I said suddenly, unexpectedly.

"Same here." Her voice had that light, casual sound it always gets when she's afraid she's getting too emotional. "I'm flying home tonight, but I'll be back next Monday."

"Think of me all the time."

Lorraine laughed. "Don't worry."

Just talking to Lorraine had a magical effect, like taking a Valium, but better. I felt calm and soothed, as though there was a future for me and it might be okay, complicated but okay. Dad will never meet Lorraine, never see me married, never see my kids, if I have them.

That evening we had dinner in the kitchen and it was almost normal. After I left, my parents ate in the kitchen more. This meal consisted of leftovers from a wedding my mother had catered. Sometimes they tell her to keep whatever is left over. So we had a lot of fancy little strange sandwiches with smoked oysters and caviar and cream cheese and some kind of weirdly interesting orange-flavored soup. Somehow, it was relaxed. We didn't talk about my father, but there wasn't that stiff, spaced-out feeling there'd been before the funeral. I talked about visiting Diamond. Mom said what a nice couple Kim and Wendy seemed to make and how fond they seemed of each other. I told her what Kim had said about Dad's influencing him to go into medicine.

"It made me feel good in one way," I said, "but bad in that I never really talked to him about what he did."

Mom made a wry expression. "Neither did I. We were married twenty-five years and I never understood one thing about what Sam did. I used to think maybe he should have married a woman doctor like Nancy Gould, but he said he liked my being part of a different world. I decided to believe him."

Kaylo was gulping down the rest of his milk. He still drinks it with Strawberry Quik. "Hey, Mom, can I go over to Andrea's now? I promised to help her with her homework."

My mother glanced at the clock. "Be back by nine," she said.

"I will." He charged off.

Mom sighed. "Should I worry about this? They're so young! At that age you were — "

"A total mess," I finished for her. "No, why worry? He's a great kid."

We cleared and when we were done Mom said, "Let's have a brandy, why don't we? I was just clearing through some things and found this incredible brandy someone gave Sam once. It was so good we never felt we had a proper occasion to use it. Brandy doesn't go bad, does it?"

I shook my head. We carried the brandy and the glasses into Dad's study. "I suppose I'll have to do something with this room," Mom said. "Or move. But I'm not going to think about that for a while."

"That's a good idea," I said.

My mother looked all around the room. "I wonder why Sam had so much trouble sleeping. It seemed to just get worse, the older he got. I always thought maybe it had something to do with his mother."

"What about her?" I asked. The brandy was incredible. I still felt calm and soothed; the light was dim.

Mom was silent for a long time. "This is something I never told you, Charles," she said. She looked at me carefully. "I don't even know if I should tell you, but I'm going to. Do you remember when Grandma died?"

"Sure."

"Sam gave her an overdose of sleeping pills. That was why she died in her sleep."

My heart flipped over. "Did you know?"

"Not at the time. He didn't want the responsibility for doing it to be anyone's but his. But I suspected something. He acted so strangely around the time of her death."

A flash memory entered my head of Josie and Mariel trying on my grandmother's clothes and my father getting so upset and then crying and Josie leading him out of the room.

179

"I think I always knew," my mother said, "because when he finally did tell me during the summer, I didn't feel at all surprised or shocked."

I realized I didn't, either. "Why did he do it?"

"Out of love. That's one thing I'm sure of. He adored her and he couldn't bear to see her suffer. He hated those nursing homes. He knew he could get away with it, if that's the right expression, because she had no money, she was elderly, he gave her just the right amount. I don't blame him. I didn't then and I don't now. I might not have been able to do it myself under the same circumstances, but I don't blame him."

I thought of my father and me visiting the nursing home, the old lady who clung to him, asking about her dead son. I thought of the beer and corned beef sandwiches we'd had in the bar, and my father asking if I could tell the difference between draft beer and bottled. "I feel the same way about it," I said. "The same way you do."

My mother reached over and squeezed my hand. "I'm glad," she said. "I'm glad I told you about it, too. I know Sam never doubted he'd done the right thing, but still I feel in some way it weighed on him. How could it not? He was such a sensitive person. I think that must be the bravest thing anyone can do, to kill someone you love to spare them suffering. My mother just asked if we could leave some pills near her bed so she could take them herself when she was dying of cancer. But that only works if the person is mentally competent, which Gustel certainly wasn't." She looked at me.

"Would you do it to me if I was in the shape she was?"

"Would you want me to?"

My mother hesitated for a long time. Then, "Yes," she said.

"I don't think I could do it, Mom," I said, as though I were letting her down in some way.

She reached over and squeezed my hand. "Don't worry, Charles. I won't hold you to it." She yawned. "Goodness, I feel so tired. Maybe it's the brandy. Usually I stay up till midnight, but lately I've been falling sound asleep by nine-thirty."

"I guess you need the rest," I said.

My mother stood up and stretched. "When Kaylo comes back, tell him I turned in, okay?"

I said I would. After my mother left, I stayed in my father's study, lying on the green velvet sofa. I began thinking about that big farm Josie had said she was going to have, in fantasy anyway. Since it was a fantasy, I made myself rich enough to buy it for her and I made my father and grandmother still alive. I married Lorraine and we had two kids, and in the summertime all of us, including my parents, my grandmother, and Kaylo, would go down there, by car probably, to visit Josie on her farm. I'd lie in a hammock under some huge spreading oak tree and Lorraine and Josie and my parents and grandmother would sit on the porch, shelling peas and talking about this and that. I wouldn't be able to quite hear what they said because they'd be a little too far away. I'd be tired because I'd have gotten up early to help Josie weed in the garden, so tired that, without even realizing it, I'd fall asleep until I heard my grandmother bending over me, calling me to dinner.

"Charles," she would call, and I'd get up, slowly, stretching, and walk to the house to join them.

NORMA KLEIN has been breaking ground in Young Adult literature ever since the publication of her first novel, *Mom, the Wolfman and Me.* Her books include *Sunshine, It's Okay If You Don't Love Me, Beginner's Love, Angel Face,* and most recently, *The Cheerleader.*

Norma Klein grew up in New York City. She received her B.A. from Barnard College and a master's degree in Slavic languages from Columbia University. The mother of two teenage daughters, Norma Klein lives with her husband, a molecular biologist, on the upper West Side of Manhattan.